This book must be returned by the date specified at the time of issue as the DATE DUE FOR RETURN.
The loan may be extended (personally, by post, telephone or online) for a further period if the book is not required by another reader, by quoting the above number / author / title.

Enquiries: 01709 336774

www.rotherham.gov.uk/libraries

DESTINY CALLING

It is 1952. William Cobridge has returned from a trip to America a different man. Used to a life of luxury, he had been sent away to learn about life in the real world. He meets teacher Paula Frost on a visit to see her aunt, the housekeeper at Cobridge House. He is keen to see Paula again and asks her for a date. Could this be the start of a new romance? But then, things never go smoothly . . .

CHRISSIE LOVEDAY

DESTINY CALLING

Complete and Unabridged

LINFORD
Leicester

First published in Great Britain in 2012

First Linford Edition
published 2013

A catalogue record for this book is available
from the British Library.

ISBN 978–1–4448–1575–7

Published by
F. A. Thorpe (Publishing)
Anstey, Leicestershire

Set by Words & Graphics Ltd.
Anstey, Leicestershire
Printed and bound in Great Britain by
T. J. International Ltd., Padstow, Cornwall

This book is printed on acid-free paper

Coming Home, 1952

William stood at the ship's rail, watching as America slipped away behind him. It had been an amazing trip, much of it good, but there had been some bad times, too, some of which had disturbed him beyond measure. But it had at least given him time to come to terms with his future.

The son of Nellie and James Cobridge, he was the heir apparent to the Cobridge china factory in the Potteries. The prospect of being a part of such an industry had been driving him crazy. In so many ways, he had enjoyed the benefits of belonging to a wealthy family all his life, even if he found his mother's side of the family less desirable.

Sheltered by his private education for many years, when he reached the age of eighteen, he was suddenly facing the

1

wider world. It might have been four years ago, but her words still came back to him. The relationship with his mother had never been quite the same since. He'd never forget those awful, tension-filled weeks.

'I would never have believed a son of mine could be such a snob,' his mother had told him.

'But there's always half your family hanging on here, and Father and I have to put up with them. His parents would turn in their graves if they saw what their lovely home had become.'

'Maybe, but times change. They lived in a cosy world of their own with everything just as they wanted it. If it hadn't been for your father and me working our fingers to the bone all these years, you'd have been working yourself by now, instead of swanning around your posh school getting fancy ideas,' his mother told him.

William didn't give up.

'But your family were only miners. One of your brothers is a farmer, and the other lives his life up to his armpits in clay. At least your sister showed some spirit and found herself a decent chap to marry.'

'Who do you think works for your father to provide him with money and keep the factory going? They are people from miners' stock and labourers,' Nellie said stubbornly. 'And if Joe hadn't been a farmer during the war years, you'd have been a lot worse fed than you were. As for your uncle Ben, he also makes a massive contribution to your father's business. Earns the company a lot of money and prestige.'

'Lizzie managed to escape getting her hands dirty,' William put in.

Nellie stared at him and laughed out loud.

'She was a nurse all through the war. Can you imagine how dirty her hands got at times?'

'At least she married the son of Sir Geoffrey and Lady Miles. It proves that she had some ambition,' William huffed.

'When you look at our background, the four of us Vale children have all done pretty well for ourselves. Made the most of what talent we have.' She paused, knowing she was making no headway with her son. Her accent had slipped back to its Potteries deep vowel sounds. He glared at her before speaking again.

'Father says I can go to university. He has fixed it for me to go to Cambridge, actually. At least then I can be among my own kind there. I can say goodbye to this grimy life for good.'

'I know all about that,' Nellie told him. 'Just bear in mind that this grimy life has provided you with all the money you need to be among what you call your own kind. I don't think you've ever been quite the same since you knew that Beth was on the way. I never expected you to be so jealous.'

'To be having a baby at your age, well, can you blame me? I have never been so embarrassed,' William complained.

'Beth is very precious. It's a pity you had to be so far apart in years as it means you'll never really get to know her. It might have done you good to realise the entire world doesn't revolve around you.' Nellie paused before continuing softly. 'Go off to your university and mix with your snobby friends, but never forget where you came from. Mining may sound like a poor sort of background for you, but I made a decent life without becoming a snob. And whatever you think, I do love you, William. More than you'll ever realise.'

* * *

Now it was four years later. William and his mother were still estranged to some extent, their differences still rankling. She'd never completely forgiven him for his harsh words that day. Perhaps now, he was beginning to understand why.

Once he had graduated from Cambridge, he'd spent six months in

America. Before he left, he'd imagined it would be a land of freedom and opportunity with limitless riches waiting to be made. The reality was very different. Despite introductions to a number of his father's contacts, who had sung the praises of Cobridge China, he had no more idea about what he wanted to do in the future.

The poverty in America was probably very similar to that in Britain among some levels of society. People seemed to rush around much more, especially in New York, and everyone seemed to shout to make themselves heard.

His father had organised that he should travel around the country so he could see more of the lives of what he considered ordinary people. There was a marked contrast between their lifestyles, with some having grand houses and others living in places that seemed to him like little more than shacks.

It had been a sobering experience that brought him right down to earth. Once he had left the sheltering presence of people who knew his father, he had been robbed. He had learned what it was like to be poor, albeit a relatively temporary state of affairs. All the same, he had been very shaken and his way of thinking drastically changed. He couldn't bear to speak of it to anyone.

He left the ship's rail and went down to his cabin. He hoped he would soon find his sea legs on this trip. The journey out had been a nightmare, with seasickness striking him almost the first day out of port. This time, he knew that he needed to control his greed and made sure to resist the delights of first-class food and excesses in the bars and dining room.

He planned to spend as much time as he could out on deck in order to get plenty of sea air. He also knew that he needed what was really the last opportunity to think about how he was going to spend his life. He would not be able to rely on his father to provide him with money for ever.

In fact, James had hinted that the family business was not doing quite as well as it had been when he had left for America. He had been given a substantial amount of money to travel around and he had accepted it as his due. But he was beginning to understand that this might have been at some sacrifice for the family, and losing a lot of it the way he had taught him a valuable lesson.

He shuddered at the terrible memories and tried once more to push them out of his mind. His father had sent him an unusually long letter, which he had received just before he had left New York for home. It was well-timed for him to reflect on it during the journey, and it had clearly set out some of the things that had given William his easy life.

'Maybe you've grown up a bit at last, William Cobridge,' he murmured. 'You really had become a snob, just as Mother said, and probably been an absolute brat for most of your life.' He felt ashamed of all the things he'd said in temper that memorable day. He had missed his mother's companionship and knew it had been a dreadful mistake to speak out that way. He also knew that she must never have told his father, as it had never been mentioned again.

Would he ever be able to make it up to her, he thought. He doubted he could be so forgiving, if the boot was on the other foot.

Looking around at the opulence of this magnificent liner, the *Queen Elizabeth*, he remembered that he was the first of the family to experience such a trip. His mother was too busy looking after everyone to contemplate such a journey. Besides, she had been the mainstay of most of the new ideas for the company, and possibly the reason for much of its success. He took out his father's letter and re-read it. Towards the end, James had made things very clear.

Whilst we will always do our best to

support you, it is time you took responsibility for your own life. I hope this trip has shown you a wider world. Enjoy your cruise home and please ensure that you understand that this is the final holiday we shall pay for before you start earning your own living. I understand that you don't want to be a part of Cobridge China, a deep sadness to myself and your mother, but I would never force you to follow a life you might hate. I hope you will be able to reach your decision without too much heartache.

Your loving father.

That was clear enough. He had to start earning a living somehow. But how? Perhaps he could be a writer like Auntie Lizzie. His degree was in English, so that was a good start. A small provincial newspaper would have no great prospects for him, but it could be a start. Perhaps he could write a book? Did people earn much from writing books? He doubted it. Besides, what would he write about? He could live at home while he wrote it, but it would mean he was still reliant on his parents. Perhaps he could take up photography?

He glanced at his watch. It was time to get dressed for dinner. He could continue to ponder endlessly, but for now he needed to be sociable. It would be interesting to meet his fellow passengers, and maybe even glean some ideas from them. This what it was all about. Meeting people and making contacts.

In his evening dress, fortunately left at his father's friend's house during his trip south, William knew he presented a fairly decent sight. He was reasonably tall and shared his father's neat, blond good looks. He accepted the proffered cocktail as he walked into the room, looking around for someone he might talk to. University had given him the confidence to mingle with large groups of unknown people, which was something he knew that his mother still found slightly inhibiting even after all these years.

He approached a group of people and introduced himself. The fact that the group included a pretty girl of twenty or so might have had something to do with his choice.

'Good evening. Excuse my presumption, but I am travelling alone and realise I don't know another soul on board. Let me introduce myself. I'm William Cobridge,' he said confidently.

'How do you do? I'm Richard Dempsey and this is my wife, Mona, and my daughter, Bella.' The accent was clearly from somewhere around the New York area. 'And you're obviously from Great Britain. How we just love the English accent, and we can't wait to visit your country.'

'Thank you. Yes, indeed, I'm from England. Where are you planning to visit?' William asked.

'We have one heck of schedule planned. We want to see everything we possibly can. And we're taking in Scotland and Wales as well,' Richard told him.

'That sounds quite a trip. How long are you staying?'

'Just over two weeks. But yours is such a small country, we're sure we shall be able to do most things in the time we have.'

William smiled and turned to Bella.

'Good luck to you. It sounds like a lot of travelling in a short time. Is this your first visit, Miss Dempsey?'

'It's my first time out of my home town,' she said with a laugh. 'I assume you're returning home now?'

'I am indeed. I've had a great time. America is truly a country of great contrasts. Some things better than others. I'm going back home to start earning my living,' he told her.

Bella laughed.

'That sounds grim. What line are you in?'

Despite his usual negative thoughts about the Pottery industry, he found himself telling them about the family business, and even felt an unaccustomed touch of pride when they showed great enthusiasm.

'Why, owning a set of English bone china is everyone's ambition where we live. Anyone who is anyone aspires to have their table set with English china,' Mona Dempsey told him. 'Cobridge? Isn't that the name of that china I liked so much in the local store, Bella?'

'It was, Mother. You raved about one of the designs in particular.' She named something William vaguely recognised.

'I think that was one of my mother's designs. She's their head designer, actually. Various members of my family work at the factory. My father is the director, of course,' he told them proudly.

'Well, now, fancy that. How very interesting to meet you, Mr Cobridge. I'd love to hear all about it.'

'Maybe we can stop by when we're visiting your area?' Mr Dempsey suggested.

William nodded eagerly.

'You'd be very welcome, sir. If you have the time, that is. You've planned a very ambitious trip for just two weeks.'

'We'll try our best to do it.' Mr Dempsey turned to his wife. 'Maybe we can even place an order for that dinner service you wanted so much, darling.'

'It would be so nice to have ordered it right from the factory where it's made,' she replied, smiling.

They all sat at the same table for dinner and by the time the meal was over, they were on first-name terms. William and Bella were planning games of deck quoits and any number of other social events that were offered.

When William arrived back at his cabin, he realised that he had spoken quite freely about the family he had pretended to despise. What was more, he knew he had spoken of his parents with great pride. His words had been accepted with a degree of admiration that was most unexpected. It gave him a whole new raft of confidence, and again he felt mortified by some of the hurtful things he had said in the past.

He fingered his father's letter again

and smiled contentedly. He was really looking forward to seeing everyone again. Even Uncle Joe and Uncle Ben and the whole assorted tribe. He still had reached no decision about his future plans, but what did that matter?

For the rest of this trip back, he was going to have fun. The rest of his life could wait.

An Old Friend

Paula Frost packed up her school bag at the end of the long week. She felt weary and looked forward to getting home. Her mum always cooked steak and kidney pudding on a Friday night and she felt her mouth watering in anticipation. She hadn't had time to eat her sandwiches at lunchtime. In fact, she'd divided them between three of her small charges, who seemed to be undernourished to a worrying degree.

She made a note to herself to look into getting subsidised school dinners for them. The dinners weren't the best, but they were nutritious and, for a child so short of food, a huge benefit.

The classroom door was pushed open. Paula turned, wondering who it could be at this time. She was surprised to see a little girl from her class standing there, looking forlorn.

'Please, Miss Frost, my mummy hasn't come to fetch me.' The little girl was tear-stained and must have been waiting in the cold for at least half an hour.

'Oh, dear, Mary. Are you sure she said she was coming? She didn't tell you to walk home with one of your friends?' Paula asked.

The child put a hand to her mouth.

'Oh, crumbs! I forgot. She said I had to walk home with Kathleen, the big girl in the top class. She lives in our street.' Mary burst into a new flood of tears.

'And did she tell Kathleen? Did she know she was supposed to take you home?' Paula asked.

'I don't know.' She sobbed. 'But I'm not supposed to cross the big road by myself. Mummy had to stay in with my little brother today because he's got a bad cold.' She sniffed again.

'Where do you live?' Paula asked with a barely hidden sigh. She would have to

18

take the child home and catch the later bus.

'At forty-one Longbridge Road, Longbridge,' the little girl recited.

Paula smiled.

'Good girl. You remembered that extremely well.' She had been teaching her pupils all to remember their addresses, and her message had got through to this one child, at least.

Longbridge Road was in the opposite direction to her bus, but there was nothing else she could do.

'Just wait a minute until I collect everything and I'll walk you back home,' she told the little girl.

'Will you, miss? That's ever so kind of you.' Mary was cheering up by the minute. Paula managed a weak smile as she put the class's books in her bag and tidied everything away on her desk. She needed to get the little girl home before her mother became too worried. Going to her own home would have to wait a while longer.

They walked the half mile or so with

Mary chatting nonstop all the way. Paula held her hand and wished her bag wasn't quite so heavy. But the chat gave her something of an insight into this child's family and could only help her to know some more of the problems her pupils faced. It was all too easy to ask the children to read to their parents every night and to get them to practise spellings, but she needed to remember that many of their parents were illiterate themselves, and perhaps were not able to help them as much as they would like to.

'Me dad was away fighting in the war nearly till I was born,' Mary told her. 'Me big brother didn't even know he had a dad till he came back home.'

'It must have been a difficult time for your mum, when he was away for so long.'

'Yes, I think it might have bin. But I wasn't here then, and me little brother didn't come till after a long time. I was nearly four when he was brought to the house. This lady came all dressed up in a blue dress with my brother in a little black bag. He was very quiet till she let him out and then did he yell.'

'I see.' Paula smiled. The facts of life could wait for a good few years yet. 'Now, this must be your road,' she said thankfully. 'You run along and I'll watch till you get home.'

'Thanks, miss. Bye.' Mary skipped off happily, turning to wave as she went inside.

Paula retraced her steps and went to wait at the bus stop. By now the bus was filling up with workers returning home and she had to stand for the journey home. Her mother, Olive, came to open the door as soon as she appeared at the gate.

'Paula, love. I was getting worried about you. Where've you been?' Olive looked at her daughter with some concern.

'I had to walk a child home. Her mother didn't turn up and she was supposed to have gone home with someone else and didn't. Now, let's have a cuppa and I can forget all about school for a while.' Paula collapsed into a kitchen chair, relieved to be off her feet.

'You must be frozen. It's turned bitter, hasn't it?' her mother commented conversationally.

'I suppose so. But it is only March, so what can you expect? Have we got the usual for tea?' Paula asked hopefully.

'Course we have. I wouldn't dare do anything else on a Friday night. Steak and kidney pudding. Been steaming away all afternoon.'

'Wonderful. I'm starving.' She smiled.

'I bet you didn't eat your sandwiches again, did you?' Paula looked away. 'So, who did you give them to this time?'

'Oh, Mum, I couldn't eat them myself when I saw those little ones half starving. I get very well fed by you so it doesn't do me any harm, does it?'

'It's not good for you to go all day without anything inside you.' Her mum busied herself making tea from the kettle resting on the hob over the fire.

When she had given it to her daughter and made sure the girl was sitting down, she went back into the kitchen to put the vegetables on to cook.

Olive did worry about Paula. She worked much too hard and she was as skinny as a lath, but she could say nothing or she'd be scolded for fussing.

'Have you had a good day, Mum? What have you been doing?'

'I went to the shops this morning. Got some nice beef for the pudding and some things for the weekend. Oh, I saw our Wyn,' she added.

'How's she?' Paula asked. 'Life at Cobridge House still suiting her? She must have been there a good few years now.'

'Before the end of the war, she started there. Eight years now. I can hardly credit it. Her Jack's bin gone nearly ten. But, she seems happy enough. Said they were all getting ready for that son of Nellie's to get back home. Snooty brat he is, says our Wyn.

He's been in America for the last six months.'

'Lucky old William. I haven't seen him for years. Once he'd left our school, he went off to that private school somewhere.'

Paula thought about the boy she'd once known. William Cobridge had been such a sweet child, but he'd gone all superior when it came to the top class. The pair of them had always vied to see who could come top of the class, and then when they'd taken the examination for the grammar school, they both passed with flying colours, as their teacher had told them proudly.

Unfortunately, they had been the only two children who had passed from their school that year. William announced that he was going to a private school and she had a place at the girls' grammar school. She had grown to miss him and the challenges they had shared throughout their primary years.

They had met once when they were

both sixteen and at the end of their fifth form. They had swapped notes about how high their scores had been for the school certificate. They were still equal. She had stayed on to do her higher school certificate, as had William.

They had met again a year later at a dance that his mother had organised for some charity. He'd grown tall and good looking. A hit with all the girls who were crowding round, hoping for a dance. He'd been quite complimentary to her, telling her how nice she looked and how pretty she had become. But then he had gone off to university and she had gone to her teacher training college and they had never met again.

She wondered what William was like now. Somewhere way out of her circle, no doubt. But then the whole Cobridge family lived in a different world altogether. No fancy university education for her. It had been a bit of a struggle for her mother during her training, but they had made it, with the aid of some grants. Now she had been teaching for two years and loved it. She couldn't have made a better choice of career.

'Gosh, that smells good. Up to your usual standard, of course.' Paula sat down to a plate piled high with the savoury pudding, creamy mashed potatoes and carrots. 'A feast fit for anyone's table. So how's Auntie Wyn getting on? Is she still cooking, or is she more of a housekeeper now?'

'Well, she was first taken on as housekeeper after she'd lost her husband in the war. At least she had a home and an income, but I doubt that it paid her very much. She had to turn her hand to all manner of things, but my sister always was adaptable. They took advantage of her, but she didn't mind.

'She says the boy still isn't working,' Olive continued. 'I bet his parents have spoiled him rotten, him being the only son. The little girl's six. Quite a sweetheart, by all accounts, but probably getting spoiled the same way that

William did. Just think, you could easily be teaching her in a year or so.'

Paula shook her head.

'They'll never send her to our place. We only get poor kids. Besides, it's a church school and their family's chapel.'

They settled down after supper to listen to the radio and read. Her mother had also been to the library, so there were some new books. Both were avid readers and their new library had proved a godsend.

As she lay in bed that night, Paula's thoughts turned once more to William Cobridge. She'd love to meet him again and see how he had turned out. But he was way out of her class now, and he was probably engaged to be married, or at least hobnobbing with some society girl with pots of money and a season ticket to all the hunt balls in the county.

Her own prospects were much less interesting. If she was lucky, she might meet someone one day, but the chances seemed increasingly remote in her present life. Romance and chance meetings just didn't come her way. She might go out more in the evenings, if it didn't mean leaving her widowed mother on her own. Mum was always cheerful and did often suggest that she should go out, but going out anywhere on her own just didn't seem like much fun.

'Why don't you go shopping today, just for a change?' her mum said after breakfast next morning. 'You could get the bus up to Hanley and have a look round the shops? You could do with something new to wear. That old skirt you wear every day is looking decidedly worn. Go on, treat yourself.'

'I might, actually. It sounds like a good idea. Do you mind if I make a day of it and have a bite to eat for lunch somewhere?' Paula asked her mother.

'Of course not, love. It will do you good to get out. I'll have some supper ready for you when you get back. Something cold so it won't spoil if you're late back.' Paula gave her mother a hug. Always so thoughtful, she almost seemed to be living just for her daughter. It made her swing between feeling guilty at times and positively trapped at others.

If she did ever find someone to love, she would find it difficult to leave her mother, and having an in-law in tow was hardly a good start to any relationship.

Hypothetical, she told herself, as it was unlikely she was ever going to meet anyone, anyway. She put on her good coat and went out to catch her bus. It was a perfect time for coffee, she decided when the bus stopped. She went into Lewis's café and rashly added a toasted teacake to her order.

'Paula? It is you. I thought it was you when you came in. Come and sit with me,' a woman standing at the counter said with a smile.

'Mavis. How lovely to see you. How are you?' Paula smiled at her old friend.

'I'm escaping for the morning.

Giving myself a proper treat. My Fred's looking after the baby while I do some shopping. The littl'un needs new clothes every five minutes these days! So, got yourself a handsome man, yet?'

Paula and Mavis were old school friends and used to see each other quite regularly until she was married and had a baby last year.

Paula shook her head.

'Never seem to have time to go anywhere or even meet anyone,' she said.

'Aren't there any marriageable teachers at that school of yours? We used to have one or two likely males around when we were at school,' Mavis asked.

'I think that was in the days when teaching was a bit more enticing. You hardly ever get any males in junior schools nowadays. Apart from the headmaster, we're all women, and he's about due to retire anyway. He's married with numerous children of his own. You'd think working with kids all day would be enough to put anyone off, wouldn't you?'

Mavis laughed.

'I might have thought twice about it if I'd realised what a lot of time babies take up. No sooner have I finished one feed and changed his nappy, it's time for another. And boiling up nappies, that's something else. The whole house stinks of soapy water all the time.'

'Could be worse. Could stink of dirty nappies,' Paula suggested.

Mavis laughed again.

'You should come round one evening and meet the little fellow. Have a bit of supper with us.'

'Well,' Paula said doubtfully, 'it's kind of you, but I'm always busy with marking and preparations. And I don't really like leaving Mum on her own.'

But Mavis wouldn't take no for an answer.

'You need a break sometimes and you can't be with your mum for ever. I could invite my brother, too. You used to like him, didn't you,' Mavis reminded

31

her with a smile.

'David? Isn't he married yet? I thought he was going out with that girl from down Stoke way?'

'That all finished ages ago. No, he's footloose and fancy free. I'll organise something soon and drop you a line.'

'Thanks. Yes, I'd like that,' Paula conceded, knowing her mother would be happy.

'You can come straight round to us after you finish school. Now, I'd better get on with the shopping or he'll be going mad for another feed and Fred will ban me from ever going out again. It has been lovely seein' you again,' Mavis told her.

'And you.'

The girls hugged.

Paula finished her coffee and tried to picture Mavis's brother, David. He was a couple of years older than them and had usually teased her whenever she went round to their house.

When she was about fourteen, she'd had a huge crush on him for several months, but with her being younger he had shown no interest in her. It would be interesting to see how he'd turned out. It might be something to look forward to.

A Rare Day Out

Paula couldn't resist a quick wander around the china department in one of the larger department stores in town. As with many people from the Potteries, she had a fierce pride in what was made locally.

Most people had some connection with one or other of the china factories. Her father had been a manager in one of the small companies that made fancy goods, as they were called.

Anything that wasn't part of table settings, vases and so on, were classed as fancies. Delicate flowers, ornaments and wonderful figurines all had their places in well-lit shelves and cabinets in the store.

Some of the fancies looked so fragile that Paula would never have dared to go near them. Her mother had one or two of these pieces at home, which her father had bought as presents a long time ago, but she never dared touch them, either. They were much too precious to her mother to take such a risk.

Her father had died when she was still very young, near the beginning of the war, and she could scarcely remember him. Her mother and Wyn had since led very different lives after they had both lost their husbands. Wyn had never had children so she had been quite content to live in at someone else's house, and so she had taken the job at Cobridge's as soon as it was offered.

Paula had visited Cobridge House once when she had been friendly with William, and she had seen some of the wonderful collections of china they had. There was supposed to be one example of every piece they had ever made.

She wandered round the store, looking at some of the new lines that were coming in. After the austerity of the war years, when no properly colourful items were allowed on the home market, it was good to see the pretty things returning to the shelves. There were some lovely things, out of the reach of many local people.

Paula returned home later in the afternoon to find her mother in the kitchen, making tea.

'Here you are, Mum. I saw these in the market. Thought they'd cheer you up.'

'Oh, how lovely,' her mother replied, taking the bunch of daffodils from her daughter. 'But you shouldn't spend your money on me.'

'Why ever not? Just a little thank-you for always looking after me so well.'

They sat by the fire with a cup of tea and chatted over their day. Mrs Frost had done very little, as usual. She'd had a cup of tea with Mrs Jones, their neighbour, and listened to the radio, but she seemed reasonably content with her life.

'It's your Auntie Wyn's birthday tomorrow. I got her a card. I wondered if you could take it round to her?' she asked her daughter.

'Has this anything to do with the fact that William is due home?' Paula laughed. 'There's no reason why you shouldn't go. Auntie Wyn would enjoy seeing you.'

'She'd like to see you, too. I only saw her yesterday,' was the reply.

'You're an old schemer aren't you?'

Olive smiled and winked.

'If some of us mums didn't do a spot of scheming every now and then, we'd never have sight nor sound of a grandchild.'

'Just you watch it, Mother, dear. I have no intention of having children. I'm a career girl. I didn't sweat and slave over my books all these years just to get married and have kids,' Paula said.

'That's because you haven't found the right man yet. Once nature takes over, you won't be able to wait, believe me.'

'Well, anyway, I haven't said I'd take the card yet,' Paula told her mum.

But she knew she would. She was very keen to see William again, but she would never admit it to her mother, of course.

★   ★   ★

Sunday dawned bright and clear. In the tiny front garden of the Frosts' house the first few stiff spikes of daffodils were bravely coming into bloom. A couple of late primroses gave splashes of bright colour against the dark earth.

Paula stood at the door with a mug of tea in her hand, enjoying the early peace of the quiet Sunday street. It was a pleasant side street, away from the terraced houses that dominated so much of the area. At least they had a little bit of a garden rather than a door that simply opened from the front room straight out on to the street. Ten minutes further away was the tree-lined road where large houses such as Cobridge House were sited.

She went back inside and saw her

mother cooking bacon and eggs, their usual Sunday treat.

'I should have bought some oatcakes when I was in the market,' Paula remarked.

'You could pop round to the bakery if you really want some. It'll be a while before this is ready.'

'OK. I fancy a couple of oatcakes.' She went out and down to the main road. The oatcake bakery was always busy on a Sunday morning, usually with a long queue waiting outside.

The bakery was a small house which had given up its front room to provide the large metal sheet, heated by gas, to cook the oatcake batter. Looking like large, grey-brown pancakes, they were a unique part of the Potteries' fare, especially for Sunday breakfast. Paula eagerly collected her packet when her turn came and took the warm oatcakes home.

'I was nearly digging into them on the way back, they smell so good.' Paula laughed. 'Doubt I could live anywhere else if they didn't have oatcakes. I bought some extras so we can have them later with some grilled cheese on top.'

'Go on with you. You're lucky you can eat anything you like and still stay so slim.' Her mother put the oatcakes under the grill to warm.

'It's all down to hard work and plenty of exercise,' she said. 'I shall probably be walking to school once the summer comes. I only need to go by bus while it's bad weather.'

'I've put Wyn's card on the side-board. There's a little present to go with it, too. I thought you might go after lunch when she'll be quieter. Mind you, if the boy's just got back, they might be having one of their family dos. When the whole lot of them all turn up it's usually quite a spread they put out, I understand.'

Paula nodded.

'Be nice for you to see William again,' Olive said with a smile.

'If they have a family gathering going on, I'm not likely to see him then, am I?

40

But I'll go whenever you think's best. I'd better get on with sorting out my lessons for tomorrow, though. I wish we could afford to buy a few more workbooks for the children. It would save me having to write out sums and things for every child, every day.' Paula went into the front room and set her things out on the table.

She would have to get it done before the table was needed for lunch. But her mind wasn't on it today. She kept thinking of the tall blond man she was hoping to see later. She daren't give any hint of her thoughts to her mother or she would immediately start running wild with her imagination.

She chewed her pencil and cursed herself, remembering how she had told off her pupils for doing the very same thing just the other day.

She gave a quick sigh and forced herself back to her work. She should perhaps look forward to seeing Mavis's brother. He was much more in her league.

A Reunion

Paula tucked her aunt's card and present into her handbag and was ready to set off.

'Are you sure you don't want to come, Mum? She's your sister, after all.' Paula gave her mother one last chance.

'No, love, I could really do with putting my feet up for a little while. My legs and back are aching something chronic.'

'You've been suffering quite a bit lately. Maybe you should see the doctor?'

'I'm not decrepit yet, my girl. It's just after the winter and the damp weather.'

Paula was having none of it.

'You're making excuses. We'll talk about it later.'

She did worry about her mother, but was always grateful that she was there and so willing to look after her. Perhaps she was taking too much for granted and should help more, not that it would be allowed by her fiercely independent mother.

Cobridge House looked lovely in the spring sunshine. It was a large, sturdy building with many windows overlooking the drive. Not just a few lonely daffodils were showing, but huge banks of them were blooming alongside the lawn. It was a sheltered garden, tended by a regular gardener and colourful shrubs and flowers grew everywhere.

She walked up the drive and round to the back door. Only family and their visitors were allowed to use the imposing front door. She knocked and waited for someone to come.

'Yes?' the maid answered.

'I've called to see my auntie Wyn. The housekeeper? I'm her niece, Paula Frost.'

'If she's your auntie, then you must be her niece.' The girl giggled. 'Come inside, then. I'm sure it will be all right.'

'Sorry, I wasn't thinking. You're new

here, aren't you?'

'I'm Sarah. Sort of a parlourmaid, I s'pose, and general dogsbody. Not that they call it that nowadays. Mind you, Mr James is still a bit formal, I suppose. Mrs Nellie's all right, and the son's not too bad, really. He's making an effort since he got back. Used to be a right snob, by all accounts.'

'My aunt?' Paula prompted. She thought this one might chatter on all afternoon if she could.

'Sorry, miss. Come on through. She is in her sitting room.'

Paula followed the girl into the large, warm kitchen, still smelling of roast meat from lunch. Sarah knocked on the door of the little sitting room at one side of the kitchen and opened it.

'You've got a visitor, Wyn.'

'Paula. How lovely to see you. Come on in. Will you make us a pot of tea, please, Sarah? And some of that cake we baked this morning, too. A couple of slices won't be missed.'

'Happy birthday, Auntie Wyn. Mum

sends her love and this card. Oh, and a little something.' Paula handed the gift to her aunt. 'So, how are you? And how's life treating you here at Cobridge?'

'I'm fine. Life is busy as always. Could do with a bit more help here, but nobody's interested in domestic work these days. Now his young lordship's back it's going to be all parties and old friends coming by.'

'I did wonder if there would be a family tea party today,' Paula said.

'No, thankfully. We had some of them round to dinner last night. That war-injured chap and Mrs Nellie's sister, Lizzie, they call her. And a couple more of his friends.'

'What's he like after his trip to America?' Paula asked, interested how William had turned out.

'You know something? I reckon it's done him a lot of good. He used to be quite demanding and rude to us servants. Never said thank you for anything. But he's quietened down now. You were friends with him at one time, weren't you?'

Paula nodded.

'Only at junior school. I've seen him a few times since, but I'd hardly call us friends. He had turned into a bit of a snob from what I heard, and felt Nellie's family were all beneath him.'

'She's an amazing woman, actually,' Wyn told her. 'She might have come from a poor background, but she runs this place like clockwork, and she runs most of the factory in the same way, from what I can make out. I've got a lot of time for her. Now where's that tea?' She opened the door and went into the kitchen.

'Are you drawing the water from the well, Sarah? We're dying of thirst in here. Oh, Mr William. Sorry, I didn't see you in there.'

Paula heard the familiar tones coming from the direction of the kitchen.

'That's all right, Wyn. I'm trying to

persuade this young woman to let me have some of that excellent fruit cake, but she says it's for tea and I have to wait.'

'I suppose we can spare a slice,' Wyn told him. 'I'll cut it up before serving it so nobody will know there's any missing. I was going to give my niece a slice, as well, so I can hardly say no to you, can I?'

'So, you have a niece tucked away in your sitting room, do you?' William peered through the glazed door into the adjoining room.

'Yes, sir. You might remember her actually. Paula Frost? I think you were at school together once,' she reminded him.

'Goodness me. Paula Frost! Of course I remember her. I should do — she always used to beat me and come top of the class. I was most upset that any girl could be cleverer than I was. I didn't know she was your niece. May I say hello to her?'

Without waiting for an answer he

pushed the door open and Paula rose from her seat. She found herself blushing with pleasure at seeing him again. He was the main object of her visit if she did but admit it.

'Paula. How are you?' He took her hand and then leaned over to softly kiss her cheek.

'William. Goodness me, You've grown even taller.' She laughed. 'You must tower over your parents.'

'You've certainly grown into a lovely woman, if I may be so personal. I hardly recognised you.'

Wyn came in with the tea tray and set it on the table. She poured out two cups and hesitated. Should she offer one to Paula first or William? They were chatting amicably so she handed one to Paula, protocol taking second place. She gave each of them a plate with a slice of cake.

'Did you know your aunt makes the best fruit cake in Staffordshire? But you have to work hard to get her to part with any of it until after my parents have eaten their fill,' William informed his old friend.

Wyn snorted good-naturedly.

'Nonsense, Mr William. You can wheedle anything out of anyone with that charm you put on. He's a real flatterer, you know, Paula. Just watch out or he'll be trying his wiles on you.'

It was a lively half hour, all of them laughing and joking together.

'You haven't opened your card yet, Auntie Wyn,' Paula reminded Wyn.

'I'm saving it till later,' she replied with a warning glance.

'What's this? A card?' William wanted to know.

'It's Wyn's birthday,' Paula informed him.

'Does my mother know? She would surely want to mark the occasion in some way.'

'Nonsense. Now you keep quiet about it. I hate any fuss.' Wyn was looking quite pink with embarrassment. All the same she reached for the card and opened it. 'Oh, that's lovely. Such pretty roses. Your mother always did choose the most beautiful cards. Please say thank you to her.'

'Of course I will,' her niece agreed. 'You're right, William, this cake is wonderful. But I should be getting back.'

'You should come to visit me more often,' Wyn said. 'And tell your mother to come round to see me one afternoon.'

'I will.' She rose and put her coat on. William leapt up to help her.

'Would it be all right if I were to walk you home?' he offered.

'Well, of course, if you really want to, but it isn't far.'

'Silly girl. I'm only doing it for myself. I wanted an excuse to spend a bit more time with you. I'll just get my coat and meet you in the hall.'

'I'll wait outside at the front,' Paula said shyly. 'I didn't use the front door.'

'Nonsense. You're my guest now. Come through when you've said goodbye to Wyn.' He went through the door and shut it softly behind him.

'Well, now, who's made an impression, then?' Wyn said with a knowing smile. Paula blushed once more.

'He's just being polite.'

'Don't play innocent with me. He likes you and you like him. You make a lovely looking couple. Enjoy the attention while it's there, my girl. Make the most of it,' her aunt said knowingly.

'Well, we'll see, won't we? Now, enjoy the rest of your day and don't forget to open Mum's present.'

Paula made to leave.

'Hang on a minute. I'll look at it now so you can tell her I liked it.' She unwrapped the package and revealed a china brooch. Tiny flowers clustered together and fastened with a pin on the back.

'Oh, but that's gorgeous. How lovely — and what a clever person who made this. Please thank Olive for me and tell her I really love it. Bye, love, and thank you for coming to see me.'

'I'd better go or William will give up

waiting for me,' Paula said.

Wyn opened the door and showed her through to the hall. William was waiting by the front door and smiled brightly as she walked towards him. It was a long time since she'd been there and she'd forgotten how grand it was, with the oak panelling everywhere and large sweeping staircase.

'This is so lovely,' she remarked.

'What? The hall? I suppose it is quite nice. I never really notice it any more,' he replied.

'Are you going out, William?' a voice called from the stairs. 'Oh, you have a visitor. I'm sorry, I didn't realise. Aren't you going to introduce us?'

'Oh, Mother. This is Paula Frost. You remember her? We were at school together, before I went to boarding school.'

'Oh, yes, I do remember. You were always quite a clever little thing, weren't you?'

Paula smiled.

'Mrs Cobridge. Good afternoon. I

was just here to see my aunt and William offered to walk me home.'

'You have an aunt here?' Nellie asked.

'It's Wyn, Mother. And it's her birthday today,' William told his mother. 'That's why Paula came to see her.'

'Oh, I'm sorry I didn't know. How remiss of me. I shall go and wish her well right away. Enjoy your walk, dear, and nice to meet you again, Paula.'

'And you, Mrs Cobridge.'

The pair walked down the drive together and were soon chatting easily. Paula found herself only half listening to his words, thoroughly enjoying being with such a handsome companion. She almost wished some of her pupils could see her now, so she could prove that she did have a life away from school. She was certain some of them thought she spent her life tucked away in a cupboard in the classroom and only came out each morning to greet them all.

'So, what do you think?' William asked, looking at her quizzically. She hadn't heard his question, day-dreaming as she had been.

'I'm sorry?'

'Will you come out with me one evening during the week?' he repeated.

'I'd like to, but I'm always very busy in the evenings. I have to prepare all my lessons for the next day,' she told him.

'Saturday evening, then. We could go dancing, if you'd like that. Or out for dinner somewhere. Or perhaps you'd like to see a movie? Sorry, a film. They call them movies in the States.'

'I'd love to hear about your trip. Perhaps if we went out for a meal, you could tell me about it?' Paula suggested.

'All right. I'll borrow one of my parents' cars and pick you up. Seven o'clock OK for you? I'll book somewhere nice. I'm still a bit out of touch, but my father will know where I should take you.'

'Well, if you're sure. But haven't you

got swarms of people to see? You've only been back a few days.'

They approached Paula's house.

'Nobody I'd rather spend time with. Now, one of these is your place, isn't it?' William asked.

'Yes, we're right here. Thank you for seeing me home. I'll look forward to Saturday.'

Paula watched as he strode away, the long legs quickly taking him out of sight. She touched her cheek and felt the warmth still there.

Her mother opened the door immediately.

'You should have invited him in. So that's the famous William Cobridge, is it?' she asked.

'Yes, that was him. Wyn was delighted with her brooch and the card. Said you always had excellent taste,' Paula replied. 'I had tea with Wyn and William. He's turned out rather well, don't you think? Much less of a snob than I was expecting. He's rather good-looking, too, don't you think?'

'Don't hold out your hopes, love. He's probably got a whole string of girls after him. He's from a wealthy family and they mix in different circles to the likes of us,' Mrs Frost warned.

'But you were the one who wanted me to go to see Wyn in the first place, just so I could meet him.' Paula laughed. 'Still, maybe you're right. But he has asked me out to dinner next week. I might just have to buy something more fashionable to wear after all.'

She went upstairs to her room, leaving her mother slightly open-mouthed. She shook her head slightly, fearful for her precious daughter. Aiming too high for a husband could lead only to heartache. Hadn't Paula said the other day that she might go to see her old school friend and meet up with her brother? That would be a much more suitable match for her. She should never have sent Paula to see her sister.

A New Frock

Saturday couldn't come soon enough for Paula. She had thought about William every day. She tried hard to keep her concentration at school, but found herself drifting off into a little dream world all of her own.

She also tried hard not to lay too much store on the coming date. As her mother had said, William was really out of her reach and would want different things from his life.

She told herself that it was just a casual date, old friends catching up on their lives. He had given her a brotherly peck on the cheek because that was how he saw her. It was probably the American influence. Everyone kissed everyone in the films she had seen.

By Saturday morning, she had worked herself into a state of complete panic. What would they talk about? Had she anything at all to say to him that might interest him? He'd never be interested in hearing about her work at the school.

The biggest question of all was what she would wear. She pulled out every item of clothing she could find in her wardrobe. There was nothing that seemed suitable for what might be a fairly posh restaurant. She didn't want to let William down or allow him to think she wasn't good enough.

'For goodness' sake, Paula. He's just a bloke. You don't need to get into such a state for a simple meal out,' her mother chided her.

'But this is the first date. Well, even if it isn't exactly a date, it's important to me, and I want to look nice for him,' she told her.

Olive took out some money from her purse and gave her daughter some notes.

'I'd rather you didn't spend it all, but use what you need to buy yourself something new to suit,' her mum said generously.

'Mum, thank you so much. I'll pay you back as soon as I get my next wage. You're wonderful.'

And with that Paula rushed out of the house and began running along the street to the bus stop. Somewhere, there was the perfect outfit waiting for her. She needed to find it and most of all, be able to afford it. She positively rushed from store to store, but anything she really liked was far too expensive.

She tried the market in desperation. The trouble was, she would always know it came from a market stall. She found a bright blue dress, with a pretty neckline and just a tiny bit of embroidery round the top. It looked quite classy and certainly not like something you'd buy from a market stall. It was a good price and would leave some change from her mother's notes.

She left it there, unable to decide. She did a lap round the market and returned to the stall only to see someone else holding on to it, clearly intending to buy it. Great, she thought. Why had she prevaricated? Suddenly it had become the one and only suitable thing she had seen all day. The other woman bought it and she had to begin all over again.

She looked at the big clock overlooking the market and felt even more pressure, as time was running out.

'Oh, William,' she muttered. 'What sort of thing would you like to see me wearing?'

'Sorry, miss, did you say something?' the stall holder asked.

'Sorry. No. I was cursing myself for not snapping up that blue dress.'

'It would certainly suit you. Lovely dark hair and blue eyes. Just your colour,' he agreed.

'I know. But someone else has bought it now.'

'It just so happens I have another. I don't ever like to put out two things the same. You ladies don't like to think someone else is wearing the same outfit as you.'

Paula couldn't believe her luck!

'Really? In the same size?'

'Exactly the same,' he told her.

'I'll take it!' she said to the man.

'I knew you would. Soon as I saw you looking at it, I thought, that's the right dress for that lovely lady. Goin' somewhere special, are you?' he asked kindly.

'I hope so. Thank you so much for your help.'

He packed the dress into a large paper carrier bag and handed it over. Paula took it and waved goodbye. She couldn't help but smile as she went to catch her bus.

'Paula. Wait.' She turned as her friend Mavis called out to her.

'Oh, hello. Twice in as many weeks. I'm just going to catch the bus home.'

'I was going to write to you, but now I've seen you, I can ask you. I was speaking to David yesterday and mentioned you. He'd really like to see you again. I wondered if you'd come round on Friday evening? You can see the baby, and David will come round for supper. Please say yes. It would be great to catch up.'

'Oh, that's really kind of you, but, the thing is, well, I've met someone. It's an old friend. We sort of met up again and he's taking me out this evening. I've been buying a new dress for the occasion,' Paula explained.

'Well, you're a fast worker, right enough. David's going to be that upset. He told me he'd always fancied you. Never liked to ask you out because you were a bit posher than us,' Mavis joked.

'He was always lovely, but I was intimidated by him being that bit older. Quite funny when you think about it. Look, I'm not sure what's going to be happening. I'll write to you if I have a spare evening coming up. What's your address?' She wrote it down on a piece of paper she found in her handbag, doubting she would ever take up the offer. 'I'm sorry but I'll have to go. My bus is just coming in. Nice to see you again.'

'And you. Have a nice time.' Mavis walked away looking disappointed and Paula felt slightly guilty. It was typical, she thought. She never went out and now she had two offers within days of each other.

She needed to get home. With any luck, she'd have time to wash her hair and have a bath before she went out this evening. She willed the bus to go faster, but it crawled along at its usual pace, the conductor chatting to every-one as they climbed on board.

By seven o'clock, long dark hair shining and her new dress neatly pressed by her mother, Paula was ready.

'You look a real treat, love. That William couldn't help but be impressed by a lovely young lady like you. He's a mug if he isn't.'

'Thanks for giving the frock a press, Mum. It didn't do it any good being crushed into the carrier. It's nice, though, isn't it?' Paula seeked her mother's reassurance.

'It's lovely,' Olive told her. 'The

colour's exactly right for you. Makes your eyes look very blue. Oh, look. Your date's arrived.'

Paula smiled. Her mother sounded as excited as she was. She went to the door and found William about to knock. He held a bunch of flowers in his hand, plus a box of chocolates.

'Good evening,' he said. 'I wasn't sure if you'd like flowers or chocolates so I brought both. You can share both of them with your mother.'

'How very kind. Won't you come in for a minute?'

'Thanks, but the table's booked for seven-thirty so we mustn't be late. It will take us at least twenty minutes to get there. Mrs Frost. Good evening.'

'Nice to see you again, Mr Cobridge — William. How lovely,' she said as he handed her the flowers. He gave the chocolates to Paula.

'Thank you, but how did you manage to get these without coupons?'

'We have our ways. Be a good thing when rationing ends altogether. Can't be much longer now. You look lovely, by the way.'

'Thank you,' she said, blushing.

They made polite conversation for a few minutes until he said, 'We really should be leaving now. Nice to see you again, Mrs Frost. I promise I'll take good care of her.'

They set off with Olive watching as they drove away. She was pleasantly surprised at his good manners, after all she had heard about him. He'd finally grown up, it seemed.

Would he be joining the family firm, Olive wondered. She rather hoped so, because if he and Paula should ever make a match of it, he would stay in the area. She couldn't bear to think that one day her daughter might move a long way away from her. It would be bad enough when she moved out to get married.

She had such mixed feelings about it. She wanted her daughter to find someone wonderful, but it would be such a wrench to lose her.

She gave a sigh and turned on her radio. There might be a nice play on this evening. Saturday Night Theatre was always one of her favourites. She filled a hot-water bottle and clutched it to her stomach, hoping it might ease the twinges she kept feeling. Something she'd eaten, no doubt.

A Wonderful Evening

Paula felt surprisingly nervous as she sat twisting her hands together in the front seat of the little car. William drove well, but she felt unsure of herself. She had never eaten anywhere really posh and this evening promised something quite new to her. Would she know which cutlery to use? And what should she order? She might not recognise what things were, especially if it was one of those places that had their menus set out in French.

'So, how was your week?' William asked. 'Did you get all your lessons written out?'

'You're teasing me. It was all OK, really. One or two of the usual problems, but nothing disastrous. How about you? What have you been doing?'

'Trying to decide what I'm going to do with the rest of my life.'

'Is that so very difficult?' she queried.

'It is. It was easy for you. I seem to remember you always wanted to be a teacher right from the start. You even pretended to be the teacher in class once.'

'Did I?'

'Oh, yes. You were very strict and told me I was a naughty boy for not doing my writing neatly enough. I expect you're even more strict now.'

'Goodness, fancy you remembering that.'

William smiled at her.

'I remember an awful lot of things about you, Paula. I've often thought about you over the years. Wondering how you'd turned out. I even wondered if you'd be married by now, with a horde of children hanging on to your apron strings.'

'But I'm only twenty-two!' Paula exclaimed.

'That doesn't mean anything. Plenty of people are married and having babies at twenty-two.'

'You're right, of course. I met Mavis Harper today. She's got a baby. Seemed quite happy, I suppose.'

William nodded and there was a comfortable silence for the remainder of the journey.

'Here we are.' He stopped the car outside the pretty restaurant right out in the country.

'This looks lovely. I've never been up here before.'

'It's one of my parents' favourite places. They started coming here a couple of years back, just for a change. Come on. Let's enjoy ourselves.'

It was a cosy restaurant with a huge open fire taking away the chill of the March evening. Tables set with white linen cloths and coloured candles on every table made it look very special. The waiter showed them to a corner table, quiet enough for them to be able to talk and look over the rest of the diners. There were still several empty tables, but it was certain they would soon be filled to capacity. They were handed a large menu each and a wine list was placed on the table beside William.

'Are your parents well, sir?' the waiter asked.

'Very well, thank you. They recommended we come here, so I hope your reputation lives up to their claims,' William joked.

'We'll do our best, sir. I'll leave you to make your selection. Can I get you a drink while you decide?'

William looked at his friend.

'Paula?'

'I'll just have some orange squash or something, please,' she told the waiter.

'And I'll have half a pint of bitter.'

The waiter smiled and went away.

'I thought we might have some wine with our meal. Do you like wine?' William asked Paula.

'Dare I admit that I'm not sure? We never have anything like that at home and I don't go out much.' She blushed as she spoke, knowing that it made her look even more gauche than she realised.

'Then you shall definitely try it tonight. Now, what would you like to eat?'

'I shall take your recommendation.' Paula felt rather uncomfortable and somewhat at a loss of what to say to this man who seemed to know exactly what to do and say. She had rarely eaten out and only then it had mainly been in cafés and shop restaurants. They simply couldn't afford anything more special, living mainly on her mother's war widow's pension and her own earnings from teaching. It didn't leave a lot left over for such luxuries.

'It must be difficult for you, with your mother to consider all the time,' William said kindly after ordering coq au vin for them both. 'She is on her own so often while you're at work, I can quite see why you don't feel you can go out much. But she must surely realise you need some life of your own?'

Paula nodded thoughtfully.

'You are quite right, but it seems mean when she has looked after me all these years and helped me get my training at college.'

'So this also explains why someone as lovely as you is still free and single,' William commented. 'I hope this isn't going to be something that stops us seeing each other as much as I hope. I really want to see a lot more of you.'

Paula felt her cheeks colouring once more and she smiled and looked down at her fork, seemingly with great concentration. She was used to her mother telling her she looked beautiful, but William? It was embarrassing, but in the nicest way. The waiter came to take their wine order and William ordered for her.

'We'll have a bottle of claret with the meal, please.'

'Excellent choice,' the waiter said as he left them.

'I bet he says that to everyone.' William laughed.

'Aren't you going to tell me about

America? I'm dying to hear about your trip. I bet New York was amazing.'

'Oh, it certainly was. You feel like an ant creeping along the ground with all the skyscrapers everywhere. The houses I stayed in were all huge and quite different to anything we have here.' He smiled as he continued. 'I was there over the Christmas period and everywhere was filled with tinsel and coloured lights. It was beautiful.'

'It all sounds quite astonishing,' Paula noted.

'There were parts of my travels that weren't quite so memorable — ones I'd rather not get into,' he confided quietly.

Paula felt the need to change the subject.

'Tell me more about New York and the ship. What ship did you come back on?'

'The *Queen Elizabeth*. It was magnificent.'

'Oh, my goodness,' she squeaked. 'The trip of a lifetime. It was named after our Queen, wasn't it? She's now

73

the Queen Mother, of course. Such a public bereavement. Very sad. I suppose the news of King George's death must have reached you somewhere?'

'Not until a couple of weeks later. When I got back to New York.'

'It's been pretty sombre here. That poor young princess coming back from her holiday to all this. She was very dignified. Makes you think, though. She's not that much older than us. Can you imagine suddenly becoming Queen?' Paula said softly.

'Not in the least. I'd insist on being called King.'

Paula hit William playfully on the arm.

'You know what I mean!' She finished her soup. It had been a slight shock to get soup that was white in colour. Her mother's soups were always brown or sometimes red, when tomatoes were the dominant taste. But it was delicious.

'I didn't think you could make soup out of celery. That was very good.'

'You can make soup out of most things, I think. My mother tells stories of making whole meals out of bits of vegetables and some old bones. I think she rather revels in shocking people about her so-called poverty-stricken past.' He paused and looked thoughtful for a moment. He had been struck by something and looked rather upset.

Paula said nothing, assuming it was something to do with his experiences, the ones he'd rather forget. One day, she would get from him this secret he didn't want to speak of. He pulled himself together and smiled.

'Now, what do you think of your wine?'

She sipped the dark liquid, looking at it through the candlelight. It was a wonderful colour, rich ruby red given a sparkle from the light. She sipped it cautiously and frowned. It was slightly bitter at first, but a second sip and she could appreciate the subtle flavour. She took another and smiled at her host.

'It's wonderful. I think I'm going to

enjoy this whole glassful.'

'I'm glad. I want you to enjoy this evening. It means a lot to me that you would come out with me after all these years.'

'I'm sure you have never had any difficulty persuading anyone to go out with you. Now, surely you had some female company in America?' Paula asked with a smile.

'Well, yes, of course. The family I stayed with had several daughters. Most of them were rather young, but all were very charming to their English visitor.' He coloured slightly as he remembered the girl on the ship coming home. Bella Dempsey.

She'd appeared to be rather smitten with him and promised to visit when they passed through this part of the country. He'd rashly promised to show the family round his father's factory and half promised to take her out for an evening. Show her something of the England that was off the beaten track. Now he had found Paula again, he didn't want to see the American girl at all. She had merely been a diversion on the long journey home.

'So, what do you think you will do? I mean you presumably have to earn some sort of living. Will you go to work at Cobridge's, do you think?'

William thought for a moment before replying.

'I'm not sure yet. So far, I've been through thinking of journalist, author, photographer and a whole lot more.'

'All very creative. Don't you share your mother's artistic talent?'

''Fraid not. I doubt I've got talent for anything really. I have a reasonable degree in English, but that hardly makes me a writer,' he confessed.

'Isn't your aunt Lizzie some sort of writer?' Paula enquired. 'I keep up with local news and her name crops up every now and again. Or you could always try teaching.'

'I'd be hopeless. I'd want to clip the brats round the ears if they didn't do as I tell them. Maybe I should join the army or something?'

Paula laughed. He watched her eyes light up with humour and her mouth crinkled at the corner quite beautifully. He reached across the table and touched her fingers.

'It's so good to see you,' he said for the umpteenth time.

'And you.' She smiled, hoping he couldn't hear her heart thumping as loudly as it was.

It was easy conversation between the two as long as she didn't probe his views on America too much. Paula quickly learned what was acceptable and what was not.

He seemed so attentive all the time and even sounded interested in what she said about her own work. Did he seem slightly perturbed about her enthusiasm for teaching? She saw him give her a frown when she talked of changes she would like to see in teaching, and how she would do things if she was allowed.

Several times, he touched her fingers

and she felt a connection between them that was quite disconcerting. Why on earth did she feel like that, just from his simple gesture of what could only be construed as friendship?

The meal ended with tiny cups of rather strong coffee. Paula grimaced slightly at the bitterness, but it was improved with the addition of a second sugar lump.

It seemed no time at all that they headed home and were back in her own street and parked outside her home.

'It's been a lovely evening. Thank you very much. The food was out of this world. I don't think I shall be able to eat again till Monday, at least,' she joked.

'It's been a pleasure for me, too. Can I persuade you to come to tea tomorrow? I can't wait for another whole week to see you again.'

'I really do have to work tomorrow. Besides, I don't want to rush things. You need to settle a bit after your trip. But it would be nice to go out with you again soon,' she said sensibly.

'We'll go to the pictures, then. Friday night? Then we can go dancing on Saturday. They have marvellous dances at Trentham Gardens Ballroom, I'm told.'

'All right then. Pictures on Friday. But let me think about Saturday. I haven't really got anything suitable to wear to go dancing.'

William sighed good-naturedly.

'Why do women always obsess about what to wear? My mother and her sister are always spending hours trying on clothes and swapping hats. Aunt Lizzie is a terror. Always borrowing stuff and changing her mind.'

'Women need to look nice all the time and be suitably dressed for the occasion,' Paula informed him with a smile.

'I thought all that was supposed to have disappeared after the war?'

'Some of it has, I suppose, but you don't realise how difficult it is for some people. Frankly, I don't have spare money to spend on clothes. Teachers don't earn a great deal and my mum's a widow.'

William looked embarrassed.

'Well, I'll settle for the cinema on Friday and we'll make plans after that. I'll pick you up at six-thirty and we can decide where to go then. I'll find out what's on and you can choose what to see. Now, do I get a kiss?'

Paula smiled. She knew her mother would be looking out for her, but she didn't care.

'I was rather hoping so,' she replied, leaning over to him. This time, it was no brotherly peck on the cheek but a proper kiss on the lips. Afterwards, he got out of the car and came round to open her door. He gave her his hand to help her out and led her to the front door.

'Thank you for a lovely evening,' he said.

'Not at all. It's me who should be thanking you. It was wonderful. A heavenly meal and gorgeous wine. I even enjoyed the company quite a bit. Oh, and thank you again for the flowers and chocolates. That was so kind of you.'

'Paula, you're a very special lady. I can't wait for the next time. Good night.' This time, where they could clearly be seen by anyone peering out, the peck on the cheek was quite brotherly.

Olive Falls Ill

Mrs Frost was eagerly awaiting her daughter's return. She still had mixed feelings about the dinner date. She very much wanted Paula to have some good times in her young life, but she remained afraid that the son and heir of the Cobridge family could lead only to disaster and heartache. Paula was such an innocent in so many ways, despite being such a very clever girl.

'Oh, Mum. You shouldn't have waited up for me. Don't the flowers look lovely? You have arranged them well.'

'So, did you have a good time?' Olive asked her daughter.

'It was wonderful. Food like you'd never believe and the restaurant was so lovely.' Her mother smiled gently, slightly irritated perhaps that her daughter rated the food so highly. She'd always prided herself on being a pretty good cook herself. She winced slightly, unnoticed by her daughter, and continued to smile and ask her questions.

'And he treated you nicely?'

'He was the perfect gentleman all evening. Very polite and courteous. It was interesting, actually. There was something about his trip to America that upset him deeply. He wouldn't talk about it. But guess how he came home? On the *Queen Elizabeth,* no less. I've seen pictures of it in magazines. It must have been amazing.'

Mrs Frost listened to her daughter's excited chatter and smiled.

'Well, I'm glad you had a good time, but I must go to bed now. I'm dropping with tiredness. Do you want a drink before you go to bed?'

'No, thanks, Mum. I couldn't manage another thing. You are feeling all right, aren't you?' Paula asked, concerned.

'Course I am. Just tired. Night, love. Sleep well.'

'Night, Mum. And you.'

She watched as her mother hauled herself out of her chair and went upstairs. She was worried. Olive was only just past fifty. No age at all, but she had begun to look older lately and was clearly in pain. Perhaps she had been selfish in going out this evening, leaving her mother alone, but she had to do something with her life before she was too old.

In any case, her mother had seemed delighted that she was doing something for herself. She was rather glad she had refused the invitation to a family tea. Who had proper afternoon tea these days, anyway? William had made it clear it was just that, afternoon tea and not a proper supper. She and her mother often had odd cups of tea during the afternoon at weekends but rarely ate anything more than a biscuit. How the other half lived, she thought as she went upstairs.

Paula lay awake for a long time. Perhaps it was the unaccustomed rich food later than she was used to eating.

But thoughts of the handsome blond man, with bright blue eyes and a ready smile, wouldn't leave her mind.

She tried hard to tell herself that he was only being polite and really just renewing their childhood friendship, but she couldn't help but hope it might grow into something more. Something much more.

On the other hand, the sensible bit of her brain told her that she mustn't let herself make more of it than it was. She was inexperienced with men. Apart from the casual friends she'd had at college, she knew very little about the opposite sex.

She'd been to an all girls' school and, being an only child, she had never known brothers around the place. Her friend, Mavis, told tales of the disgusting messes her brother, David, left everywhere. She used to moan about him all the time. He expected to be waited on, just as her father did.

Paula hadn't known her father very well, what with him working hard when she was small and then going away to war. It must have been terrible for her mother, losing the man she loved. There was not even a proper grave to visit and leave flowers. She had been told that a cross marked the place where he lay, or might have lain if they could be certain it was him, but that never really helped. Nor did a name on some war memorial somewhere. None of it could make up for the reality of the man she had lost, like so many war widows.

★ ★ ★

Sunday morning was wet. Paula awoke late, her head aching and feeling heavy after her lack of sleep. She went downstairs in her dressing-gown, ready to apologise to her mother for being late. But the kitchen was silent. She looked outside in case her mother had gone out to fetch some coal, but the door was still locked. Suddenly apprehensive, she rushed upstairs to her mother's room.

Pale faced, her mother lay against the pillows, lifting a tired hand as Paula came in

'Mum? What's wrong? Are you ill?'

'I'm not sure. I feel sort of weak. I tried getting up but I was dizzy so I thought I'd lie still for a minute. I must have dozed off again. I must get up now or the meat won't be cooked for lunch.'

'Nonsense. You'll stay right where you are. Forget the meat and anything else.' Paula put her hand on her mother's forehead. She was very hot and damp with perspiration. 'You've obviously got a temperature. Stay there. I'll go and make some tea and then we'll decide what to do with you. You really do need to see a doctor.'

'Don't fuss. I'll be all right in a minute. Just been overdoing things a bit lately.'

'Nonsense. That doesn't give you a temperature.' Paula went down to the kitchen and put the kettle on.

She didn't know what to do at all. Her mother was always the one who always knew the right thing to do, except when it came to herself. Now it was down to her.

She could easily cope with a class of lively seven-year-old children, and even knew how to handle children who were sick, but when it was her own mother, she felt totally at a loss.

When the tea was mashed, she poured out two cups and took them both upstairs. Her mother was trying to sit up as she went into her bedroom. The effort had caused a new film of sweat to form on her forehead.

Paula put the cups on the bedside table and helped her mother up, plumping the pillows to support her.

'Sorry, love. Can you pass me that cardi? I feel quite chilled.'

'Stop apologising. Here you are, though I'm not sure how you can feel so cold when you're burning up,' Paula stated.

'Must be a touch of flu, I reckon.'

'Maybe. But you haven't been sneezing or coughing have you?'

'Not really.'

'And do you have a pain anywhere?'

'Not exactly a pain. My stomach feels a bit sore, but it's nothing really. I must have eaten a bit too much for supper last night.' It was a lie in fact, as Olive had felt unwell much of the day yesterday and had eaten nothing. She had said nothing as it would have spoiled Paula's evening out and she could never have allowed that.

'Stop making excuses, Mum. I doubt you ate anything at all, knowing you. You've been losing weight for some time now. I should have said something earlier. Oh dear, why ever did I go out last night?' Paula berated herself.

Olive spoke up quickly.

'Now stop it. You're a very loyal girl, always thinking of me and hardly ever going out of an evening, like you should be doing. Now are we letting that tea go stone cold or am I allowed to drink it?'

Paula passed the cup to her mother and watched as she bravely sipped it. She could tell she wasn't enjoying it and after a few minutes, she removed the cup from her mother's shaking hands. She swallowed her own tea as she watched her mother's face, her expression giving little away.

'I'm going to get dressed now and then I'll make some breakfast for us,' she told her mother.

'I couldn't eat a thing. Please don't try to make me.'

'How about a slice of toast? Or a boiled egg?'

'No thanks, love. Really, I don't want anything. Look after yourself and eat properly,' Olive told her.

'I might just have some toast. I'm still full from that lovely dinner last night. If it had been you eating all that rich food, I'd have said that's what was wrong. But it's something more serious, I know it is. You've been feeling more tired each day, lately. And you haven't wanted to go out shopping as much as usual,' Paula said.

'I know. Just leave me in peace now. And stop nagging me.' Olive's eyes began to close again.

Paula dressed quickly and brushed her hair. She splashed cold water on her face, letting that pass as a wash for once. She glanced in at her mother before she went downstairs and, seeing her looking as if she was asleep, she went into the kitchen and made herself some toast — more to give her something to do than because she wanted it.

She took one bite and decided it tasted like cardboard. What should she do? She wondered whether to telephone Wyn for advice, but it would mean leaving the house and going to the phone box at the corner of the road. Mind you, if she wanted to call the doctor she would have to leave her mother alone, anyway. Thank goodness she had refused to go to tea with William and his family, she thought for the umpteenth time.

She looked out of the window and saw her neighbour scurrying past, head down to avoid the steady rain. She called out to her.

'Mrs Jones? Can you spare a minute?'

'Hello, Paula, love. What is it?' The older lady stopped at Paula's voice, looking concerned.

'It's Mum. She's really ill and I don't know what to do. I don't know what's wrong with her, but I think it must be something serious. You know what she's like.'

'What do you want me to do?'

'I was wondering if you could just stay in the house with her, while I go and call the doctor?'

'I'll have to get the family sorted with breakfast first. I'll be with you as soon as I can manage it. Keep your mum warm and don't worry. We'll soon get her sorted.'

'Thank you very much.' Paula closed the window and went back upstairs. Olive hadn't moved. She lay slumped against her pillows, leaning slightly to one side.

Paula went to her mother and touched her forehead again. Her breathing was ragged and her mother seemed not to notice she was there. She went downstairs again and looked in her mother's address for the doctor's phone number. She noted it on a slip of paper, checked she had the correct coins in her purse and waited for Mrs Jones to arrive. As soon as she heard the door open next door, she rushed to let her in.

'She seems to be deeply asleep, but I'm afraid she's really sick. I'm really wondering if I should call an ambulance right away. What do you think?'

'You really need the doctor to see her first,' Mrs Jones suggested.

'Yes, right. I'll see what he says. Won't be long. She's in the front bedroom. Thank you,' she called over her shoulder as she rushed out.

She ran along the street, splashing though puddles so her feet were soaked. She pushed her way into the phone box and quickly dialled the number.

'Doctor Anderson? It's Paula Frost, Poplar Street. It's my mother. She's ill and I don't know what's wrong.'

'Slow down, Paula. In what way is she ill?'

'She's running a high temperature and she seems to be only semi-conscious.'

'And was she showing symptoms before?'

'Not really. She has been very tired lately, but we assumed she'd been overdoing things. Said her tummy was a bit tender but not really painful. I'm so worried.'

'I'll be round in a few minutes. Keep her warm and try not to worry.'

Paula put the phone down quickly, anxious to get back. She hoped the doctor remembered where they lived as she ran back, knowing she hadn't given the clear, full address. Still they must have records, she comforted herself.

Mrs Jones opened the door for her.

'You poor thing. You're drenched. Go and change out of your wet things or you'll be getting a chill yourself. I'll put the kettle on, shall I?'

'Thanks. I'll hang my coat in the scullery. Let it drip. Is she awake?'

'No. I looked in on her and she still seemed to be asleep. Don't worry. She is breathing all right,' Mrs Jones said with a comforting smile.

Paula changed her shoes, stockings and her soaked skirt. She looked at her lovely blue dress hanging in the wardrobe and remembered the previous evening with William. It seemed a lifetime away already.

Her mother remained just as she had been for the last hour.

Mrs Jones handed her a cup of tea, sweetened to give her energy, she was told. Paula grimaced. She never took sugar normally, but she swallowed it gratefully, while she looked out of the window for the doctor. His car stopped outside and she rushed to the door.

'Come in, Doctor. She's upstairs.' She led the way up and opened the bedroom door. 'She's still asleep. Can I stay while you examine her?'

'Of course. I'd want you to. Mrs

Frost? Can you hear me? It's Doctor Anderson.'

Olive stirred and opened bleary eyes.

'Doctor? Why are you here?' she whispered.

'Paula is worried about you. Now, do you have any pain anywhere?' the doctor asked.

'Stomach a bit tender. Head aches.'

He pressed her stomach gently and she groaned with pain. He pushed a thermometer into her mouth and took her pulse.

'No, don't try to speak. Just keep still.' He read the thermometer and nodded. 'Yes, as I thought. Raised temperature and a fast pulse, rather thready. I'm afraid we're going to need to get you into hospital. Have you got a telephone in the house?' he asked Paula.

'No. There's a phone box at the end of the street. Shall I go and call them?'

'No, I'll do it. They won't take long if I order it. Now, pack a few toilet things into a bag and another nightie. Slippers.

97

Dressing-gown. You know the sort of thing. I'll see you at the hospital later. You'll be able to ride in the ambulance with her.'

'What do you think is wrong with her?' Paula asked, worried.

'It might be her appendix or something else. I can't say without a proper examination,' he said.

The rest of the morning passed in a blur. Paula had barely finished packing her mother's bag when the ambulance arrived. Lace curtains twitched all along the street and the bell rang out and they set off at quite a pace. Had she locked the door? Paula wondered as she left. Never mind, Mrs Jones would do it if she hadn't.

Sitting in the cream and dark green corridor outside the admissions ward seemed to last for an eternity for Paula. The hospital smell seemed to have invaded her every pore and she was feeling sick with anxiety. Starchy nurses walked past her and doctors in their white coats came and went. Doctor

Anderson had not yet appeared as promised, but perhaps he had just been making polite comments to ease her nerves.

She began to wish she'd brought her schoolwork with her, if only to alleviate the boredom. At last a doctor came out to her.

'Miss Frost? I'm afraid you mother needs an urgent operation. We believe she has developed some sort of blood poisoning, possibly because of a rupture in or near the uterus,' the doctor told her. 'We are going to perform surgery, and she will need a lot of care and medication, but we are confident she will pull through. You can go and see her now. We shall be operating as soon as we can prepare the theatre.'

'Oh, dear. Is it going to be a difficult operation?' she asked, concerned.

'It's fairly major, but quite a common one. The toxicity is causing something of concern to us, but there are powerful drugs we can use. Go and see her now, while you can.'

With tear-filled eyes, Paula went into the ward. She tried to wipe them away with the back of her hand and fixed a smile on her face.

'Well, now, Mum. You are giving us all a shock. Are you feeling all right now?' Stupid question, Paula realised too late.

'I'm cross with you for making such a fuss,' Olive murmured.

'You needed someone to fuss over you. This must have been going on for ages and you kept it to yourself,' Paula chided her.

'Didn't want to worry you. You have your own life to live.'

'Oh, Mum. My life would be nothing without you to nag me. Just lie back and get yourself better,' Paula told her firmly. 'I'll manage just fine.'

'But you can't even cook. You'll never eat properly.'

'Stop it, Mum. I'll be fine. Anyway, it's about time I learned how to look after myself. And I'll look after you when you come home.

'Now, you're going to be very sleepy this afternoon so I'm going to go home and get everything sorted out. I'll go and see Wyn as well, and let her know what's happening. She's sure to come and see you one afternoon when I'm at work. Just stop fretting and get better. Understand?'

Olive nodded.

'Yes. love. I think they must have given me something. I feel very sleepy. You go home and put that meat in the oven. I don't want to hear it's gone off.'

'I will. Take care. Night, Mum.'

'Night? I didn't . . . ' but she had fallen asleep. Paula dropped a kiss on her forehead and walked to the door as they wheeled a trolley beside the bed.

'Please, God, let her be all right,' she whispered as she left.

Unexpected Visitors

Paula waited for a bus outside the hospital, her mind whirling at the unexpected turn of events. You simply never knew what was waiting round the corner. This time yesterday, she'd arrived home excited with her new dress. It had only been a few hours since she was sitting with William in that lovely restaurant, and even less since he had kissed her.

She must remember to tell him that she couldn't go out with him on Friday. Everything had changed now. She planned to go straight to Cobridge House to break the news to her aunt, and then she would go home and cook this wretched piece of meat her mother was so concerned about. Perhaps Wyn could give her some advice.

She must make sure her aunt passed a message to William about their date to the pictures. She would need to be at the hospital most evenings. For once, the pupils might have to take second place and learn to use the blackboard more.

She walked up the drive at Cobridge House, noticing that there were two extra cars parked outside. It must be the family tea party William had mentioned. She hoped Wyn wouldn't be too busy to speak to her. She went round to the back door and knocked. Sarah opened it.

'Oh, hello. You come to see your auntie again? Come in. She's in the kitchen rushing round like a crazy thing, she is.'

Wyn looked surprised to see her.

'Paula? Why didn't you let me know you were coming? I'm afraid cook's gone off and unexpected visitors have turned up for tea. I've got to make a heap of sandwiches I wasn't expecting. Sarah, put those things on the trolley. And then look into the oven to make sure the scones don't burn. Honestly, this lot will finish me off. Give me five minutes, dear, and I can chat to you.'

'Is there anything I can do?' Paula offered.

'No. Sit yourself down. You look terrible. Are you all right?'

'Concentrate on your tea party and I'll tell you after.' She sat in the corner out of the way and watched as the two women scurried round getting everything ready. It was all alien to her, how everyone had to do everything just so, for a family who probably sat on their backsides all afternoon. William among them, probably.

'They've only gone and invited a lot of Americans without telling me in advance.'

'They'd met Mr William,' Sarah explained. 'Came back on that cruise liner with him. Pretty girl, the daughter. They're going to visit the factory tomorrow. They want to buy some of the china to take back with them.'

'You listen to too much idle gossip, my girl,' Wyn told the maid.

'I just like to know what's going on. I think the girl's a bit sweet on Mr William. She keeps making doe eyes at him,' Sarah said.

'What do you know about doe eyes?' Wyn snapped.

'Saw it at the pictures. She sort of looks like this.' The girl put on a soulful expression and tilted her head slightly.

Paula smiled but her heart was thudding quite painfully. So William had an American admirer who had actually come all the way over to visit him. Just showed, she should never trust anything he said. He must have known she was coming and just think, she might have been sitting in there with them all, trying to be polite.

If she didn't have news for Wyn, she would have slipped away before she had to listen to any more gossip. She tried to push away her bitter disappointment, but she had too much else to think about at this time.

At last, Sarah wheeled away the

loaded tea trolley and Wyn breathed a sigh of relief.

'Oh, dear. The scones. I forgot to send the scones.' She lifted the scones on to plates from the cooling rack and put them on plates. She collected a butter dish, spooned jam into another dish and loaded them all on to trays. 'Be an angel and carry one of them for me.'

'But I can't. I mean . . . '

'Don't worry. Sarah will take them into the drawing room if we hand them to her. Nobody has to see you.'

Paula picked up one of the trays and followed her aunt, nervous in case she came across William and his American lady friend. Wyn pushed the door open and took the tray into the room. She nodded to Sarah to collect the tray from Paula.

William looked up at precisely the wrong moment and saw her standing outside the door. He opened his mouth to speak and met her eyes and saw she was shaking her head. He got up and went over to her.

'What are you doing here? Aren't you going to join us? Come and meet everyone.'

'Certainly not. Look, I have to go. Please, leave me alone. Pretend you haven't seen me.'

'But I don't understand.' William was confused.

'I'm here with some bad news for Wyn. Oh, and Friday night — I'm sorry but I won't be able to see you after all. Feel free to invite your American friend out instead.'

'Paula, what are you talking about? Come back here.'

But Paula had run away down the corridor. Shaking slightly and very close to tears, she waited in the kitchen for her aunt. Everything in her life had changed in one fell swoop. Moments later, Wyn came into the kitchen.

'What on earth was all that about? Hey, you're crying. What's happened?' she asked her niece.

'It's Mum. She's been taken ill. She's

in hospital and she's having an operation. They say there's something that's maybe poisoned her blood. She's so ill, Wyn. I'm really scared.'

'Oh, my poor love. And there's me chatting on about a wretched tea party. You should have said right away.'

'You didn't give me a chance,' she said, half laughing, half crying.

'No, I didn't. But it was something more. You were upset when Mr William came out to speak to you.

'He's a liar. I should have known better. Mum warned me. He's always had exactly what he wanted all his life. He took me out for a marvellous meal last night and said he wanted to see me again and tried to make several dates.'

'That's good, isn't it?' Wyn asked.

'Not really. He lied to me about not meeting anyone special in America and now she's come all the way over here to be with him. Just shows, you should never trust anyone.' She sniffed.

'I'm sorry, love. I don't know what to say. But tell me more about your mum.

What went wrong?'

Paula told her aunt as much as she could about the dreadful morning.

'They told me to go home and ring up in the morning to see how the operation went. Oh, Wyn, she looked so dreadful. She was so pale and lifeless. I'm really scared. I couldn't bear to lose her.'

Wyn nodded sympathetically.

'Of course you couldn't. None of us could. But she's a fighter. She'll pull through, you just see. She'll need a lot of looking after, though. Recovery can take some time after an operation. You need to be prepared for that. I hope they'll send to her a convalescent home after she's through at hospital.'

'We can't afford anything like that.

'Good old National Health Service. They should do it all without any cost to you. Don't worry yourself unnecessarily. I've got some put by should you need it. I don't spend much, with living in here. Who's going to look after you?' Wyn wanted to know.

'It's about time I can look after myself. Which reminds me. Mum was worried I should cook the Sunday roast she'd bought. How do I do that?'

Wyn gave her clear instructions and told her to put potatoes round the meat to roast halfway through.

'Mind you, you need to get it going soon if you're going to eat it tonight. It'll take quite a while. I bet you haven't eaten a thing today?'

'Well, no. But I had a big meal last night,' Paula admitted.

'Get off home now and put that meat to cook. We don't want you falling down with lack of good food. Can you take the day off tomorrow?'

'Course not. There'd be no-one to look after my class. I'll go straight to the hospital after I finish and I'll let you know how she is. Maybe you can go and see her, too, one afternoon?' Paula asked hopefully.

'Course I will. And I might even give the hospital a call myself. Mrs Nellie will let me use the phone here if I ask.'

'Thanks, Wyn. I'm glad I could talk to you.' She gave her aunt a hug and let herself out of the door. She glanced at the parked cars as she left and once more cursed herself for being a gullible fool over William. Men like him should never be taken seriously.

She could barely have reached the end of the drive when William tapped on the kitchen door and came in.

'Where's Paula?' he asked

'She's left. Gone home,' Wyn answered.

'Oh, no. I really needed to speak to her. How long ago did she leave? Might I catch up with her do you think?'

'I doubt it,' Wyn fibbed, assuming her niece didn't want to see him. 'She has problems. Her mother's been taken into hospital. She's very ill.'

'I see. I'm sorry to hear that. But I needed to explain something to her.'

'Well, your explanations will just have to wait, won't they?' Wyn was annoyed on Paula's behalf and had no time for the man who seemed to have upset her niece so much.

'I hope her mother is all right. Offer her my sympathy if you speak to her. I'll catch up with her another day.' He paused and turned back to Wyn. 'Oh, is that why she's cancelled our date for Friday evening? Because of her mother?'

'I couldn't say. It may also have had something to do with your visitor. The American girl.'

'Who, Bella?' William frowned.

'Is that her name?'

'Oh, but she's nobody. Her family were travelling over on the ship at the same time as me. They wanted some china and to see the factory.' He left the room, not wanting to allow Wyn to see his blushes.

He and Bella had been good friends on the ship, but that's all it ever was. A shipboard companionship. He'd curse if it ruined his growing relationship with Paula. He had high hopes of a romantic future with her. He went back to the drawing room, his mind far away from the niceties of Cobridge House.

'Is everything all right, honey?' Bella asked. 'I'm hoping you're gonna give us a personal tour tomorrow.'

'You'll do better to follow either of my parents round. I hardly know the place at all. I wonder if you'd all excuse me?' He couldn't bear to sit being polite. He needed to see Paula. 'I have something . . . somewhere to be. Excuse me.' He made his blundering exit, leaving Bella bereft, his mother slightly bewildered and his father positively furious. James did not want to be here with these people, but someone had to show good manners. And now he was saddled with them for the next day.

'So, tell us where you hope to visit after you leave us tomorrow?' he asked politely.

'We're doing North Wales and then moving on to the south of the country the day after. There's a lot to see. If we can make an early start tomorrow, we hope to be away by mid-morning.'

'I see,' James said in relief. 'It will

have to be a quick tour then. If you choose what you want in the way of your china, I can get it packed and sent directly to your home address.'

'That would be just wonderful,' Mona Dempsey said happily. 'If we can afford it, I'd like a table setting for twelve. Not that we entertain greatly, but with china like this, I think we may begin having regular dinner parties.'

'Now,' Mr Dempsey broke in, 'we should leave you good folks in peace. We plan to visit Barlaston next, to see the new Wedgwood factory.'

'Well, I hope you enjoy it there. We'll see you in the morning. Early,' Nellie said politely.

She ushered them out and handed them their coats along with all the other paraphernalia they seemed to have brought with them. After they'd gone, she went back inside and she and James burst out laughing.

'Americans,' she muttered. 'Fancy 'doing' Wales in a day. One thing's for sure, those folks won't want to hang

114

about for too long tomorrow.'

'Thank goodness,' James said. 'What was all that about with William? After all, they are his friends.'

'Goodness knows what goes on in his head. But he does seem like a totally different person after his trip. Has he talked to you about it?' Nellie asked her husband.

'Not a word. I know he spent a great deal of money over there, but I haven't seen the evidence. Perhaps he bought something that hasn't arrived home yet,' James replied.

'I don't think so. You don't think he's bought a property out there? I've heard there are some bargains if you look. I'd hate it if he went to live so far away. Even if he does infuriate me at times.'

'Who can tell with him. I must have a serious talk to him, though. He needs to decide soon how he will support himself for the rest of his life.'

'We will help him all we can, won't we?'

James nodded.

'Of course. But I'm not prepared to keep paying for him to laze around all the time. It's a waste of a good life and a good education.'

'We can always find something for him to do at the factory, if he wants it. He's been seeing that girl he went to school with. Paula something. Wyn's niece.'

'Is he now? And is she quite suitable for him?'

'He seems to like her. I think she's a teacher now. Sensible girl. Pretty enough, but I don't expect it will last. She's a bit too quiet for him, I should think.'

Nellie might have felt less sure if she had seen her son rushing along the road to Paula's house. William had decided that he couldn't let things rest like that. She was clearly upset at finding Bella and her family were visiting. It had been quite unexpected and he felt awkward and embarrassed to see them again.

Though he'd partly invited them

himself, he had not expected them to turn up like that. Nor had he expected to see Paula standing there outside the door, tea tray in hand like some sort of maid. He needed to put things right before it was too late.

* * *

William knocked at the door and heard a clatter from inside the house. A red-faced, flustered Paula opened the door. She was wearing an apron that was much too large for her and her hair was hanging untidily round her shoulders.

'William. What on earth are you doing here?'

'I needed to talk to you. Please, can I come inside? It's chilly here on the doorstep and people might overhear. I've already seen curtains twitching,' he told her. 'Please, let me in. Are you all right? You look upset.'

'I am. I've got a monster piece of meat to cook and I don't know where to start. Wyn said I needed to put it in the roasting tin and put it in the oven for two hours.'

'And you dropped the roasting tin when I knocked at the door. Now the meat's all over the floor and everything's ruined. It's all my fault.' Despite herself, she managed a small smile.

'I dropped the tin before I'd got it out of the cupboard. I pulled everything else out as well. It's all over the kitchen floor.'

William grinned.

'Then let's put it right. Come on. It needs to go in the middle of the oven. You turn the oven on to warm and I'll put the meat in the tin. Where's the salt and pepper?'

'On the shelf,' she muttered in surprise. How did he know anything about cooking? They'd always had cooks to do it for them at Cobridge House. Expertly, he shook seasoning over the meat and put it into the oven.

'Shall I peel the potatoes?'

'In the vegetable rack by the sink.

Knife in the drawer.'

She watched, fascinated, as he peeled potatoes, cut up carrots and chopped cabbage.

'So, are you going to tell me where you learned to do all of that?'

'Long story. I used to like watching our cook when I was a kid. She let me help sometimes. Came in useful at one time in America. But that's something I still don't want to talk about.'

'So, what was so urgent that you came rushing round here to tell me?' Paula wondered.

'It's Bella. I needed to explain. I met the Dempseys on the way back. I didn't know anyone on board the ship and they took me under their wing. They asked about Cobridge china and I invited them to look at the factory, never believing they'd find their way to us, let alone turn up for tea on a Sunday afternoon.'

Paula nodded her understanding.

'I knew Wyn was a bit put out that there were extras suddenly arriving.'

'So, am I forgiven?' William asked with a faint smile.

'I suppose so. But I still can't come out with you on Friday. I shall need to visit the hospital.'

'Why don't I come and fetch you from school and drive you to the hospital, after a bite to eat somewhere. Then we can go to the pictures after that. I can wait in the car while you visit,' William suggested hopefully.

Paula shook her head.

'It's very kind of you, but I couldn't put you to all that trouble.'

'It's for me just as much as you. I'd like to help out a bit, while I still can. Now, I was hoping to be invited to stay and eat with you.' William glanced at the huge amount of potatoes he had prepared — far too much for one person.

'Well, if you haven't had a meal, of course you can.'

'Oh, I had a roast with the family at lunchtime, but I've always got room for more.'

He smiled at her, touching her hand affectionately. She felt tears burning again, but she was so grateful to him. It would have been a much more terrible evening if she'd been on her own.

A Special Request

The meal had turned out surprisingly well, thanks to William's most unexpected abilities in the kitchen. They sat at the kitchen table and Paula even managed to relax. They had almost finished when there was a knock at the front door. It was Mrs Jones.

'Hello, dear. I wondered what had happened at the hospital,' she asked with concern.

It had started raining again, so Paula felt obliged to let her in.

'She's had an operation,' she told her neighbour. 'But there was some sort of infection, too. I'm to phone in the morning to see how she is.'

'Oh, no. I am sorry. Would you like me to come and sit with you? I can spare an hour now the children are in bed. You mustn't brood,' Mrs Jones offered.

'I've got a friend with me, thank you.'
The sound of dishes being collected
came from the kitchen. William must be
clearing the table.

'And this friend? Anyone I know?'
Mrs Jones was most curious. She'd
never seen any of Paula's friends call
round.

'Possibly not. It's really kind of you
to be concerned. I'll let you know when
there's any news.' She was trying
desperately to see her out, but Mrs
Jones was trying equally desperately to
see who this mysterious friend was.

'Well, if you're sure. Anything you
need, let me know.' She was peering
over Paula's shoulder, still trying to see
who was in the kitchen.

'Thanks very much for your help this
morning. Good night.' Paula finally got
Mrs Jones outside and went back into
the warm kitchen. 'That would be my
reputation shot if she'd seen you.
Mother goes away and I immediately
allow a man into the house.'

'I promise I'll creep out with my head

covered in a shawl or something.' He smiled.

Paula returned the smile.

They sat by the dying fire and sipped mugs of coffee. Not tiny cups like the previous night, but decent-sized mugs they usually used for tea.

It was nice to chat about their lives and things they had done, though she felt her life hadn't been nearly as exciting. William commented on the fact that she didn't have a phone in the house, and promised to help, for which she was very grateful.

His stories of punting along the river at Cambridge sounded wonderful and he promised to take her there one day. She had seen pictures of the wonderful old buildings and could imagine how it must be to experience the carols from King's College each Christmas Eve. They always listened to the broadcast on the radio.

'Oh, I've never actually been there, as I was always home for Christmas. Goodness, my mother would never have forgiven me if I'd missed the celebrations at Cobridge House. This year was the first time I've ever missed it.'

'It must have been amazing to be somewhere so grand as New York. There's always a smell here in the Potteries. Smoke, chemical stuff and a sort of greyness everywhere,' Paula pointed out.

She was struck by a sudden thought. It was already nine o'clock and she hadn't prepared her lessons for tomorrow.

'Oh, William. I'm sorry, but I still have to prepare tomorrow's lessons. You'll have to leave.'

'I could help you,' he offered, but Paula frowned.

'It's really not possible, I'm afraid. I have to know what each child can do and write them work they can manage. It's complicated.'

'That's terrible. So you have to slog away every night writing stuff out for thirty or more children?' he asked, feeling sorry for her.

'That's about it. And if I don't start doing it right now, it will take me until after midnight.'

'It isn't right, all the same.' He looked thoughtful. It surely couldn't cost so much to buy proper worksheets or books. He would speak to his father to see if they couldn't think of something. 'Well, if you're sure I can't help, I'd better leave you. Skulk out by the back door so the neighbours don't talk. Am I allowed a kiss before I leave?'

'Just one, then I must get on.'

He pulled her close and kissed her gently on the lips. With no-one watching, she allowed herself to draw close to him and felt a strength coming from him that made her feel safe and protected. It was a lovely feeling.

She let him out of the back door and unbolted the gate into the alleyway. She watched his athletic figure stride away and waved as he turned the corner.

She bolted the gate shut and went back inside, ready to tackle the mound of washing up, her mind drifting back to the handsome man who'd just left her. She tried to think sensibly. She was only a temporary part of his life, she felt sure. Hard to concentrate, it was almost midnight before she had finished her work and she fell into bed, sleeping dreamlessly in a state of complete exhaustion.

★　★　★

Paula made her call to the hospital from the telephone box on her way to work the next morning. Nervous fingers dialled the number the hospital had given to her.

'She's as well as can be expected,' the nurse told her. 'The operation went reasonably well, but there were some complications.'

'What sort of complications?'

'If you'd like to come in later, the doctor will explain things to you.'

'Mum is all right, isn't she?' Paula was getting a horrible feeling.

'She's very poorly just yet. But we hope she will make a complete recovery, given time.'

'I'll see if I can get away a little early this afternoon, then. Give her my love and say I'll see her soon.' The pips signalling the near end of the call went as she was speaking, so she hoped her final words had been heard. It certainly would be good to have a phone at home. It would save such a lot of time and provide a feeling of security. She rushed along the road to catch her bus.

It was difficult to concentrate, and at break-time, she went to see the headmaster to ask if she might leave twenty minutes early at the end of the day.

As usual, he was sitting by his desk with a heap of papers in front of him. She saw him reach down to turn one over when she went into his office. She had found out that there was a bus that went to the hospital, leaving slightly earlier than the end of school. If she could catch it, she could be at the hospital before the doctors went off duty. He peered over his glasses and looked irritated by her request.

'Is this just a one-off request?' he asked.

'Well, yes. I hope so. My mother is seriously ill and I have to speak to her doctors.' she told him.

'I see. Well, all right. I'll stand in for you just this once, but don't let this become a regular thing. And I hope it doesn't mean you'll be asking for time off when she gets out of hospital.'

'I certainly hope not, sir.'

She left the headmaster's study, fuming inside. How dare he be so rude? So unsympathetic? She worked harder than most of the other teachers and had always been totally dedicated. Leaving fifteen minutes early hardly made up for the many evenings she had stayed late to make sure everything was in good order for the next day.

William had been quite correct. It certainly wasn't right that she should have to write out individual lessons every day, especially seeing the long row of new-looking books on the headmaster's shelves. She could bet he hadn't bought them with his own money. The school budget must have been seriously depleted buying that lot. They might have plenty of new ideas about education in them, but for whose benefit? Goodness, she was becoming seriously grumpy about things.

At the end of her day, Paula collected her things together and waited for the headmaster to arrive to take over her class. Ten minutes before the end of school, he arrived, looking irritated.

'Most inconvenient,' he muttered.

Paula didn't stop to say anything and almost ran across the schoolyard. She was going to be pushed to catch her bus. As she rushed out of the gate, someone hooted from a parked car. She stopped to look.

'William? What on earth are you doing here?'

'I thought you might like a lift to the hospital. Save you catching buses and rushing. Looks as if I'm too late to stop you rushing.'

'It's very good of you, but you shouldn't have worried. I have to see the doctors before they go off duty.' She looked back and saw the headmaster peering out of the window, straight at her. Oh, dear. Now he'd think she'd made an excuse just to see her boyfriend.

'Thank you, anyway. It's a kind thought. I'm going to be in trouble tomorrow, though. The headmaster's watching me, and he saw me get into the car. He was very cross and quite unpleasant because I asked to leave early to catch the bus.'

'I thought he was nearly due to retire, from what you said the other night,' William said.

'If he isn't, he certainly should do. Do you know, he's got pounds and pounds worth of books on his shelves? I suspect that's why there's no money left over for our classrooms,' she said angrily.

'I was thinking about your problems. If you used some stiff cards, you could write out your lessons on that and pass them on from one child to the next, then you'd only have to do it once. They could copy the sums into their books themselves.'

'I had thought of doing that, but the card is too expensive and not durable enough. I'd have to buy it myself if I wanted to use it. I didn't see why I should.'

'Well, I took a chance and brought you a whole packet from the factory. My mother uses it all the time for her designs. She could easily spare you a pack of it. It's on the back seat,' he told her.

Paula looked round.

'Gosh, that's wonderful. Thank you so much.' Paula was grateful for his kind gesture.

'It might also mean you have time to come out with me more often.' William smiled brightly at her.

At that moment the car pulled up

outside the hospital and Paula got ready to get out.

'Well, thank you. I hope I won't be too long. There are no official visiting hours today,' she said.

'Don't hurry yourself. Make sure you know exactly what's happening. I'll have a stroll around the grounds and look out for you.'

The Doctor's Verdict

The same disinfectant smell assaulted Paula's nostrils when she went inside. Why did hospitals have to smell like that, she wondered again. She followed the signs to her mother's ward, expecting to be challenged by one of the staff at any minute, asking why she was there on a non-visiting day.

The ward sister came out of her office as Paula approached.

'Miss Frost?'

'That's right. How's my mother?' Paula asked.

'She's very poorly, I'm afraid. She's still sedated so probably won't have much to say to you. I'll call the doctor to come and speak to you, but if you'd like to sit with her for a few minutes, I'll fetch you when the doctor arrives. She's behind the screens at the side there.'

Paula went cautiously to pull the

screens to one side. She was not prepared for seeing her mother looking so terribly ill, an oxygen mask over her face. She sat down gently, taking the pale hand in her own.

'Oh, Mum. I'm so sorry I didn't realise how ill you were. I was so wrapped up in my own life, I didn't take the time to notice how poorly you were getting.' Olive's eyelids flickered and a faint smile of recognition flitted across her pale face.

'Paula,' she whispered, muffled by the mask.

'Don't try to speak, Mum. It's all right. I'm just here to hold your hand for a few moments. The doctor is going to explain things to me. I'm fine and quite able to manage at home. William kindly drove me here this afternoon in his car. It was so kind of him. No, don't say anything.' She knew she was prattling on, but it was all she could think of doing. There was something about hospitals that took away any semblance of normality.

There was movement outside the screens and the ward sister came through.

'Get some rest now, Mrs Frost. And Miss Frost, the doctor is waiting in my office. You can go through.'

'Thank you. I'll see you soon, Mum. Try to relax and let the nurses do their job. Love you, Mum.' Olive's eyes flickered and again there was the ghost of a smile.

The doctor, a comforting, grey-haired man, was sitting at the sister's desk.

'Ah, Miss Frost. Your mother is progressing as well as we could hope. When we operated, we found several diseased areas and there was some other damaged tissue. We hope that we have found everything and, hopefully, the powerful antibiotics we're giving her will help clear up any further infections. The next few days are critical.'

'Oh my goodness. Is it cancer?' Paula gulped as she said the dreaded word.

'We're doing tests on some of the

tissue we removed. But there are several things we can do. New treatments available to us. We shall know in a day or two.'

'How long will she need to stay in hospital?' Paula asked, trying to hold back tears and failing.

'That depends on her progress, of course. But you should be prepared for it to be several weeks, at least. She will need care when she does come out. There are people who can help you with details when the time comes. Speak to the ward sister when you need to.'

'Thank you, Doctor. And thank you for looking after my mother.'

Paula left the office and went back into the ward. The ward sister was speaking to a couple of the nurses, but she came over to Paula as soon as she saw her.

'Your mother is sleeping now. The best thing for her. I suggest you leave visiting her for a couple of days as she needs as much rest as possible.'

'I couldn't come during the afternoon anyway. I'm a teacher. I was
planning to come in the evenings when
I can. My aunt, Mum's sister, will come
one afternoon, I expect,' Paula told her.

'As you like. Try not to worry. She's
in good hands.'

It was a great relief to see William
waiting by the car. A relief not to have
to go home alone, and especially not to
have to wait for buses. It wasn't raining,
but it was dull and there was a definite
chill in the air.

The house felt cold and unwelcom-
ing when they got back. She wasn't
used to coming back to an empty
house. William carried her bag and the
pack of card and asked if there was
anything he could do to help.

'It's been so kind of you to help as
you have done, but I need to get the fire
going and organise my meal. Then I
really do have to do my school work.
I'm feeling quite exhausted, too, so I
want an early night,' she told him.

'If you're sure. I'll see you again

soon. It will be easier once I've got a car of my own. I'm hoping to persuade the old man to buy one for me, but I know I've had a habit of taking things for granted in the past.'

Paula gave a weak smile.

'I'll see you soon and we can talk then. I'd like that.'

He kissed her as he left.

At the gate, he turned and called to her,

'I spoke to the telephone company today, by the way. They will be in touch. Apparently they have just released some new numbers so you could be getting a phone quite quickly. I also told them of your situation so they'll hurry it through as fast as possible.'

'Thank you again. That's wonderful.'

Paula went back inside and fought with the fire for a few minutes before she could get it started. She hadn't cleaned out the ashes yesterday so it was a long job.

What had William said about taking things for granted? Even during school holidays, Olive was always up early and had the fire going and tea brewing before her daughter was even awake.

She made a resolution to make sure she was more help to her mother in future. Tears filled her eyes as she prayed there would be a future. She was beginning to dread the possibility that her mother may not recover. How could she manage to live her life without her beloved mother? Being just the two of them for so long had given them a huge bond of friendship, as well as their mother and daughter's love. Suppose she didn't get over this?

Her mood was interrupted by a knock on the door. She wiped her eyes, leaving a sooty trail on her cheeks.

'Oh, Mrs Jones. Come in. I'm just getting the fire going but it's refusing to draw properly.'

'You should put a piece of paper in front of it to draw it. Here, let me show you.' Mrs Jones covered the entire opening with a sheet of newspaper, leaving a gap at the bottom. It was soon roaring up the chimney and Paula could see flames trying to grasp at the paper.

'Be careful. The whole thing's going to catch fire.' Her neighbour whisked away the hot paper and folded it with a knowing smile.

'Matter of knowing exactly when to stop, dearie.'

Paula was immensely grateful, already feeling the heat begin to fill the room.

'It all looks rather dangerous, but it works, so thank you. That looks more cheerful right away.' There was a pause. Clearly Mrs Jones was waiting to be offered a cup of tea but Paula needed to get on.

'Thanks very much for coming round. I'll let you know when there's any more news.'

'All right, dear. If you're certain you'll be all right. Give me a call if there's anything I can help with. I'll be shopping tomorrow, too, if you need anything.'

Paula smiled.

'That's kind. I'll check what's in the cupboard and let you know. Now, if you'll excuse me, I have a load of school work to do. I'm quite behind with everything.'

Paula opened the packet of pristine white card. She fingered the smooth texture and could see it was top quality and much more expensive than anything she could have afforded for her class. She wished there was some way to protect it, but she would warn the children to make sure their hands were clean and woe betide them if they scribbled on the sheets.

She decided to make a start on writing out the cards immediately. She became absorbed in her task, enjoying the feel of writing on something decent for once. Her writing was always neat and her cards looked most professional as she completed sheet after sheet. It was after seven o'clock when she realised she was feeling very hungry.

She prepared her meal following William's instructions. The memory of their shared meal came back to her. Were they going steady? She really didn't know what that meant. They were certainly seeing each other quite often, but it was hardly a romance, was it? Yes, they had kissed a few times, but she was determined she wouldn't try to make of it something more than it really was.

William was being very kind and supportive, but their lives had been so very different since their primary school days. He'd lived an exciting life and travelled right across the ocean and seen America. How amazing was all of that? Her longest journey had been to Prestatyn in North Wales, for a summer holiday five years ago. It was the only holiday she could remember, apart from day trips around this area.

No, they were certainly not going steady, her and William. She was probably just a diversion for him during this time while he was deciding his future. The thought was slightly depressing.

James's Joy

William was thoughtful as he drove back from Paula's house. He stopped the car in the drive and went inside the house.

'I'm back, Mother. Hope I haven't kept you waiting,' he called. Nellie came out of the drawing room wearing her hat and coat.

'I am now quite late for my meeting, William. I hadn't realised you were going to be out for so long,' she said with a frown.

'I'm sorry — Paula has got such problems. I really needed to help her out. She was kept waiting for ages at the hospital and I could hardly abandon her,' he said by way of explanation.

'Well, no, I understand that, but we shall have to see about getting you your own car. Once you decide what you are going to do. Give it some thought, please. Now I really must go.'

'Thanks anyway, Mother. Have a good meeting. I'll talk to Father when he gets back.'

He went into the kitchen to see Wyn and tell her the latest news of Mrs Frost, such as it was.

'Any chance of some tea? And something to feed a starving man?' he asked politely.

Sarah was standing near the range and put the kettle on to the heat, giggling as she did so. She liked this handsome son of the family and even tried a bit of harmless flirting with him.

'You're always hungry, Mr William. Whenever we see you it's because you're hungry,' she said, giggling.

'It was all the years away from home. You've no idea how we were half starved all the time. I need to make up for it.'

'Rubbish,' Wyn snapped at William sarcastically. 'I used to help pack up your tuck boxes. You had more goodies in them than the family ever had.

'Now, what's the latest news of my sister? I heard you were taking Paula to the hospital.'

'There's not much news, but I gather things aren't too good. Paula was most upset when she came out. But she wouldn't say very much. She said she had to phone tomorrow and her mother isn't to have any visitors for a day or two. She needs rest.'

'Oh, dear. I should go round to see Paula. She'll be quite lost without Olive looking after her,' Wyn said sympathetically.

'She sent me away this evening. She wanted to do her school work. I don't understand why she has to work so hard. She should be out having fun at her age.' William shook his head.

'Oh, I do agree with you, but she's very dedicated to her pupils. I think she must be a very good teacher, from what I hear. Now, is that kettle boiling, Sarah? I can find a piece of flapjack if that will be enough for your poor starving condition,' Wyn offered William.

'You're a treasure, Wyn. That would be wonderful. You may be responsible for saving my life, single handed,' William told her.

'Sit down then. I'm not carrying a tray upstairs when you've come in so late for tea.'

* * *

They chatted comfortably at the kitchen table. Sarah was hovering around, hoping to be noticed, but William was keen to talk to Wyn about her niece.

Despite the string of eligible young ladies his parents always seemed to parade before him, it was always Paula that had fascinated him most. It was Paula who always crept into his mind at odd moments, disturbing his thoughts even when he was trying to reach some sort of decision about his future.

'Thanks, Wyn, and you, too, Sarah. I should let you get on. Isn't Cook here today?' William asked once he had finished his snack.

'She's got a week off. Meals are down to me at present,' Wyn said.

'I'm sure it will all be lovely. It's a good job that my parents don't have a major dinner party this week. Thanks again.'

William went to his room, still thinking about Paula. He hoped they might even have a future together. He liked the idea of settling down with her. He may not be very old, but a few more years were never going to make any difference. He'd taken out any number of girls at university, some he'd rather forget about, but none of them made him as content and happy as Paula did.

It had made him realise one thing. Whatever work he did, he wanted to stay somewhere nearby so he could continue to see her. Might he possibly consider marrying her? It was an interesting thought.

William realised he couldn't make that sort of decision until he had his own income, and it was still all very new. But he had always thought about her over the years as the one female with whom he always felt completely comfortable.

Although he had always resisted it, working for Cobridge's seemed like the only realistic option at present, but he had no artistic talent, nor any skills on the manufacturing side. In fact, he was a pretty poor specimen when it came down to it. So much for a good education. He would speak to his father as soon as possible and see if there was an opening for him somewhere within Cobridge China.

He knew his father would be delighted to have him working in the company but he needed a proper job and not just something created for the son of the owner. James had always seen it as a heritage thing, a company passed down from father to son.

William had heard hints of this from being a very small child, but as he'd grown, he had shown little interest in any of it. He'd scarcely visited the factory since he was about ten years old. Everyone had made a fuss of him at the time, but he hadn't liked the chemical smells and the eternal dust lying everywhere.

What could he do? Perhaps he could work on the sales side? Surely it shouldn't be too difficult to sell such attractive china. Everyone knew about it and he'd always heard complimentary things said about his mother's designs.

Once he was established, he might see about courting Paula properly. He might actually have something of his own to offer her. Dear Paula, he thought fondly. She was a real genuine, caring person. He hadn't come across too many of her sort outside the family he had once pretended to despise. He felt immense shame once more for his unkindness to Nellie. How terribly hurt his mother must have felt.

* * *

After dinner, William asked his father if he had time to talk.

'Certainly, my boy. If it's about your future, your mother should also be present.'

'I'd like to see Beth put to bed first, if it can wait for a while,' Nellie said.

'Of course,' William replied, though he knew he would have found it easier to speak with just his father. He was sure his father would understand more about how he felt. Was he ready yet to talk to them about his American experiences?

He shuddered and decided against it. He might never be able to speak of it to his parents. He fingered the now almost healed scar which nobody had noticed since he returned home.

It was at least an hour before Nellie came down again. James was already waiting in his study, as was his habit after dinner.

'Where's William?' she asked.

'I suppose he's gone to his room. I'll call him,' Nellie said.

'Just a minute. Do you think he's made some sort of decision? About what he wants to do?' James asked hopefully.

'Lord knows. Who can tell how that son of ours thinks? I sometimes can't believe he's the same boy who left us four years ago. I'm certain something must have happened in America. And clearly, it was something unpleasant and it has shocked him into behaving decently at last,' Nellie put in.

'That's a bit tough, isn't it?'

'Well, he had been behaving quite atrociously for some time. He said some extremely nasty things about my side of the family and, well, he was being a total snob. There's been tension between us for some years,' Nellie went on sadly.

'He's coming down now. We'll see what he has to say for himself.'

William entered his father's study and sat down opposite his parents.

'Mother, Father. I think it's the right time to discuss my future with you. You have been extremely generous to me all my life. I realise that now and I apologise that I always took so much for granted. I think that it's about time I began to work. I've been wondering whether you have a position of some sort for me in the factory, Father? I'm not sure what yet, but perhaps you can advise me?' William asked.

James beamed delightedly.

'That's wonderful, my boy. Everything I've always hoped for, but I never wanted to influence you one way or the other. That's wonderful, isn't it, Nellie?' James looked to his wife.

'I'm sure it's what you've hoped for. But what are you thinking of doing, William? How do you see your career progressing?' Nellie asked.

'I'm not sure.'

'You don't exactly display any talents on the creative side,' his mother pointed out.

'I'm sure we'll find something,' James was saying, consumed with his delight in welcoming his only son into the fold.

'Perhaps you can become my assistant,' he said brightly.

Nellie snorted gently.

'How? What do you need assistance with?' Nellie questioned him.

To Nellie, James's role seemed to be ever diminishing. He was still the managing director, of course, but lately, he seemed to be little more than a figurehead. There were managers in each of the departments and a large sales team, too. Where her husband had once led sales, especially to the export markets, he now relied on his team, and as far as she could make out, he spent a lot of his time shuffling papers.

James frowned at his wife. He heard the slight note of scorn in her voice. He had to confess, if only to himself, that she did have grounds for saying it, but he had always defended himself most strongly. He knew he was now in the position his father had reached.

A man at the head of the company who actually did very little more than socialise with local businessmen and people in similar positions to himself. He knew that he was responsible for appointing a capable workforce. Delegation was the key to a happy, unstressed life.

'Perhaps he could become part of the sales team?' James asked his wife.

His wife nodded, considering this idea as James continued.

'We need fresh marketing ideas, that's for sure. We haven't really made progress since before the war. We've been coasting along on our reputation and things are changing in the industry.'

'Surely that was because of the war?' Nellie pointed out sensibly. 'Quite a number of established companies didn't manage to survive the war years with all the restrictions on materials and the work our people were actually allowed to produce.'

James had always felt they had been very lucky and knew that was mostly because of Nellie's persistence.

'I was thinking about the Coronation.

It will be next year, won't it?' William suggested.

'I believe so. They are still deciding on which date. What's your thinking?'

'Well, surely it will be a terrific opportunity to manufacture some new lines. Memorabilia. Souvenirs. You know the sort of thing,' William said, growing more enthusiastic.

'Not really our style,' James replied. 'More the sort of thing the fancies makers will be doing.'

'But we already have several lines we could use. We could adapt cups and saucers. Jugs. Plates. Slap a royal badge of some sort on it. Put gold edges round them and you're away.'

'You've really thought about this, haven't you?' Nellie said with pride in her voice. She was actually quite surprised he should have taken this on board.

William smiled and shrugged. The truth was, he'd only just thought of it as he was speaking. But if it fitted the plan, fine by him.

'Your mother's in charge of this sort of thing. But if she thinks it's a good idea, we'll certainly look into it,' James told his son.

'Come into my office tomorrow,' Nellie told him. 'We'll discuss it properly. If you can do some research into the badges, as you call them, and come up with costings and some firm ideas, we can look at a marketing role for you.'

'Thanks. That would be great. I really want to settle down now. I want to work for my living instead of relying on handouts. I want to be able to buy a car as soon as possible and, well, I have lots of other plans, too,' William said vaguely.

'And would Paula be a part of these plans?' Nellie asked shrewdly.

'Maybe,' he replied, colouring slightly.

'You've been seeing quite a lot of her lately.'

'She's needing some support at present. Her mother, you know. But I'm very fond of her. A very different background to me, of course, but she's a deep thinker and very bright. She got better results than I did in the school certificate.'

Nellie smiled at her son's obvious affection for the young girl.

'Don't be in too much of a hurry to commit yourself, dear,' she warned. 'Now, you also asked about a car. It will be some time before you earn enough to buy one for yourself. Do you think we might buy something for him, James? Something small so he can get himself about. Then I shall stand some chance of having my own car available when I need it.'

'Gosh, that would be terrific, Mother. Thank you.' William was all smiles.

'It's only a suggestion at the moment. We'll give it some thought,' James spoke again.

He was beginning to feel left out of decision making and reflected that this was how his own father must have felt as James had grown up and moved into management at the factory. He'd only let go when he had become ill towards the end of his life. But James was barely fifty himself, and not ready to be consigned to the scrap heap just yet.

Perhaps having his son working alongside him would provide new inspiration.

'I'll see about getting that old office next to mine cleared out for you,' he said. 'It's not very large, but I'm sure it will be satisfactory.'

'Thank you, Father. It will be good to have something positive to do. I also really need to get acquainted with the work that goes into manufacturing. I've always rather shied away from it.'

James was positively beaming. William was saying all the right things and proving he was serious.

Nellie remained a little sceptical. How much of this was just a whim of their son's? Was he just saying the right things for the right reasons? Or was he trying to ingratiate himself with his father to get something he wanted? Like the car, for instance?

She gave a small smile to encourage the two men as she listened to them making plans and suggestions. She felt marginally guilty at her disloyal thoughts, but she had always been immensely practical and was usually very shrewd in her dealings with people. How else had she risen from a lowly maid in the house to be James's wife and a director of one of the most prestigious china manufacturers in the country?

Her reputation in the industry was on a level with many of the great names, but she had never once forgotten where she came from. The trials she had suffered when growing up were very much a part of her and had made her what she was today. But James and William had much the same background. Relatively easy lives, a good education and high expectations that things would come easily to them. Well, good for them, she thought.

'I'll have a word with Tom at the garage. See if he hasn't got a suitable runabout for you,' she put in.

160

'Thank you very much. That would be terrific,' William replied brightly.

'Do realise that when you start work with us, you won't be able to rush off to see Paula at four o'clock each day,' Nellie told him.

'You should bring this girl to meet us,' James suggested. 'If you're spending so much time with her, we should get to know her. Make sure she is a suitable person to be seen with you.'

William exchanged a glance with his mother. She wouldn't like that comment, and may well see it as fitting in with her definition of snobbery.

'I'm sure she's a perfectly respectable girl. Wyn is a very straight sort of person, so I expect her niece comes from similar stock.'

'She's lovely, Mother. Very well brought up and quite dedicated to her work.'

'Perhaps she won't ever want to leave her work if she's so dedicated,' Nellie said warningly.

'I haven't ever discussed such things

with her. We haven't been seeing each other for all that long. But she is certainly the nicest young lady I know, and we do go back a very long way. Well, thank you both for listening and for making a wonderful offer.'

'We'll see how things work out,' Nellie said cautiously. 'You'll be working for a living, you understand that.'

'I wouldn't want it any other way,' William replied.

He rose and left his parents, knowing they would want to talk things over.

He could see his father's enthusiasm and was also aware of his mother's caution. He was embarking on something that would take him a lot of time before he could really prove his worth.

He gave a shudder, remembering once more the sights he had seen in America. That alone had made him realise that so many things he had taken for granted were also things he should always cherish.

He wondered what Paula was doing. He would have liked to go and talk to her about his future, but it was possibly too soon. The plans might be little more than ideas at present, but he sensed that if his father had anything to do with it, he was already seeing a secure future. It was his mother he would need to convince.

He went to the kitchen to see Wyn, for no real purpose other than as an excuse to talk about Paula.

★   ★   ★

Nellie and James remained in the study, talking through the plans.

'I'm just delighted with his attitude,' James was saying over and over. 'And he seems to have some good ideas, doesn't he?'

'You need to be a little cautious. Something has obviously changed his views about the factory, but we mustn't have too high an expectation of him. Let him find his feet before we get too carried away. I haven't forgotten some of his comments about the factory before he went to university. It was all very much beneath his aspirations and he saw us all as very inferior beings.'

'He was young then. Still finding his feet,' James defended his son.

'Nevertheless, some things he said were unforgivable, even for a young man.' Nellie shuddered, remembering the argument.

'I knew things were tense back then, but whatever did he say that upset you so much? They are things that have obviously stayed with you all this time,' James observed.

'I don't want to talk about it. There were things said about my family in particular. Hurtful things that I know were partly true. But you have always managed to spend time with them, welcome them here, despite the fact they came from such a different background to you. I suppose it rankled because I suffered the same way when we were first married. Your mother was quite terrible to me. She always made me feel as if I'd crawled

164

out from under a stone.'

'And Lady Miles was the same with Lizzie, wasn't she? She never believed that Lizzie was a suitable wife for Daniel,' James put in.

'You're right, but with Daniel being so badly wounded, I suspect she was glad to get him off her hands, if the truth be told. We're a strange lot, aren't we? My brother Ben married to Jenny, the former nursery maid here. Brother Joe married to Daisy, a farmer's daughter.'

'But they inherited the whole farm when Daisy's father died. Your brother has done rather well for himself,' James said.

'Oh, he certainly has and he's very happy. But we were all the children of a simple coal miner and came from the poorest background you could imagine. Or maybe you couldn't imagine it.'

'You are all great people,' James said. 'I may not always have been at ease with the family en masse, but I'm proud to be associated with them. And

165

though I don't say it often enough, I do love you, Nellie. And I'm so proud of you and what you've achieved.'

'James,' she said fondly. 'You're the one who believed in me and gave me my chances, right from the start. You encouraged me in those early days. Do you remember the shocked looks you got from everyone when you gave me paint and papers and sat me in the little room next to your office? I remember the housekeeper was most upset.'

'Oh, yes. Mrs Wilkinson. She thought I'd gone mad.' James laughed.

'I had to sneak off and paint in secret whenever I had any time. Then you moved me to the factory and I had the little room next to your office.'

'And now our son is going to take over the same little room as his own office. You know, I can see a bright future for Cobridge China now.'

Nellie nodded.

'We shall see. But don't build your hopes too high. I'm sure something happened in America. Something that has affected him deeply. So much so that he is willing to forget all the terrible things he said about our factory and people living up to their armpits in clay.'

'He said that?' James was shocked. 'I'm not surprised you were irritated.'

'That was only a part of it, but it's the part that most affected me,' Nellie told him, before continuing with a smile. 'I could do with a brandy. Shall I pour one for you?'

'Why not? Let's go and sit in the drawing room and relax for once.'

'We don't do it often enough. I was thinking of inviting Lizzie and Daniel to dinner soon? Shall we have a family do or invite a few people?'

Nellie loved any excuse to invite guests. She had hated James's dinner parties at one time, but now she positively relished them. It was the confidence of reaching middle age and knowing who she was and being happy with herself.

'Let's make it a bit of a party to

celebrate William becoming a part of the company. We should invite the Bradleys and their daughter. She must be about William's age. Nice girl, as I remember,' James suggested, warming to the idea.

'I suspect William would want to invite his Paula. It would be a chance for us to meet her,' Nellie told him.

'But is she suitable? I mean, will she cope with a dinner party here?'

'And now who's being a total snob?'

'Sorry, dear. I'm only thinking of her. I don't want her to feel uncomfortable.'

'We'll have to wait for a while. Cook's on holiday. It isn't fair to put it on to Wyn. Especially while her sister is so ill. We could invite Paula to tea first, so we can decide what she is really like and whether she will cope with a more formal occasion,' Nellie suggested.

'Won't it be awkward for Paula, coming as a guest if her aunt works here?'

'Bit like me waiting at table and then marrying you? And the famous time

Lizzie stood in as waitress for Jenny at a dinner party so Jenny could keep her date with Ben. You'd be amazed at how well we women cope with these situations.'

'I don't think I have heard about the Lizzie story. You must tell me some time,' James said with a smile.

Nellie smiled and leaned over to kiss her husband lightly on the cheek.

'Oh, I will. Now, let's have that brandy.'

Hard Work Rewarded

Though her mind continued to race late into the night, Paula managed to get a period of decent sleep. Worried out of her mind about her mother, she tried hard to concentrate on her work for the day.

She was up early to organise the chores before she left, so that coming home in the evening might be less stressful. She wasn't expecting to see William again for a few days, as they hadn't made any plans. She would do more work on her cards this evening and be ready to spend time at the hospital when she was allowed to visit again.

The inevitable report from the hospital was 'as well as can be expected.' What did that mean, she wondered once more. What exactly were they expecting in the first place?

She caught the bus, deep in thought. She went straight into her classroom to get everything ready for the arrival of the children, but was interrupted by the headmaster.

'Miss Frost. Perhaps you can explain yourself? I saw that you were met at the school gate last evening. A gentleman in a car. You clearly told me you needed to catch a bus to the hospital, necessitating your leaving early. I was most inconvenienced at having to take your class for the latter part of the day.'

'I'm sorry. I was planning to catch the bus, but my friend came to collect me. It was completely unexpected and had I known in advance that he would be there, I should not have needed to trouble you.'

'Then why did you not return to complete your duties?' he asked.

'Because it was almost time for the bell anyway. You were only there for ten minutes at the most.'

'You are being impertinent, Miss Frost. Sadly negligent regarding your duties to your class.'

'I'm sorry, sir, but that is not fair. I work extremely hard to give my pupils the very best help under difficult circumstances. We cannot provide them with the books and the worksheets they require, so I have to work long hours every evening to make sure they have material to work with.'

'Part of your duties, Miss Frost. If you are so unhappy with the work here, then I suggest you might do well to look for another position.' He turned angrily and swept out of the room.

Paula felt like crying. He was an odious man and had no understanding of his staff or sympathy for the pupils. He came from a different era, it seemed to her, and was quite out of place in this deprived school. It was surely time he was thinking of retiring. The staff all worked hard for the sake of the children who lived in such a poor area.

She looked at her set of pristine work cards and, once more, a flood of resentment for the criticism swept through her. But she drew a deep breath and tried to calm herself as her pupils filed into the room.

'Good morning, everyone,' she said, calling them to order.

'Good morning, Miss Frost,' they chanted back.

'You can sit down now. Today, I have something special for you.' She held up the cards to show them. 'I have made some work cards for you. What you have to do each lesson, is to copy the sums from the cards into your books and then you can work out the answers for yourselves. You must never write or draw on these cards as each of you will have them in turn.'

'Did you make them especially for us, miss?' little Mary asked.

'Yes, I did. And I plan to make lots more for sums, as well for your English work.'

'That must have been hard work, miss. They're very nice.'

'It took me a long time, but then it takes me a long time each day to write things out for you all in your books,' Paula explained.

'Please, miss, thank you, miss. Nobody ever did nuffin like that for us before.'

Paula smiled. She wrote sums out in their individual books every night, but they didn't seem to realise it. But somehow, the children could always make up for the unpleasant things in life. She forgot the headmaster and his nasty comments and got on with her day.

'Now, don't forget what I said. You mustn't write on the cards.'

She called out each child in turn and handed them the appropriate cards for their ability.

It was lovely to see the looks on their faces as they carried the cards carefully back to their seats with almost an air of reverence. She saw once more how much these children were deprived of good things, and made a vow that she would try to bring pretty things in for them to look at.

Perhaps William would drive into the

country so she could pick wild flowers for them and they could draw them in the art lessons. William. She thought of him so often, but now it was because of him her class were all working quietly this morning. A little gift of some card had meant so much to them all. When she collected the books to mark, she saw that they had tried very hard to write more neatly than usual. It was an interesting result.

There was no staff room at the school, but the other four teachers sometimes had their lunch together in one of the classrooms. Paula told one of her colleagues about the earlier encounter with the headmaster.

'He more or less told me to look for another job,' she said miserably.

'He's an embittered old fool,' her colleague suggested. 'You're brilliant at your job. Probably the most conscientious one here. He must have got out of bed on the wrong side.'

'I noticed he has a new collection of books on his shelves. Shame we couldn't have some new ones for the classrooms. I've made some work cards for my lot. A kind friend donated some new card,' she told them.

'Comes to something when we have to rely on that sort of thing. I'm in a desperate position with paints, too,' another teacher put in. 'There's so little left, I have to limit the colours the kids can have. And paper, too. They just get small pieces now instead of the lovely big sheets they used to have. Nothing we can do about it.'

'Could always make him a 'happy retirement' card and hope he gets the message.' They all laughed but, in truth, it was a bad situation.

'I'm certainly not going to abandon my little lot,' Paula said fiercely. 'Unless he forcibly sacks me, I'm staying here.'

'Good for you. We're all behind you. We'll go on strike if he does that.'

Paula avoided seeing the headmaster again and was relieved to reach the end of the day without further argument. The support of her colleagues meant a lot to her and she went home in a slightly happier frame of mind.

As she reached the telephone box, she decided to call the hospital again. This time, the message was less bland and the sister sounded somewhat concerned.

'Should I come in to see her?' Paula asked.

'Tomorrow would be a good time. She is still rather sleepy at the moment. Complete rest is what she needs,' the sister told her.

'I'll come right after I finish work. Thank you.'

She put the phone down and stared at the instrument, wondering if she should telephone Wyn and ask if she could pass on a message to William. He might be able to help her with transport. Perhaps she should call round to see Wyn rather than telephone.

She let herself into the cold house and put the kettle on. It had been quite a difficult day but she relaxed, thinking of the children's delight at seeing their new work cards. Poor little mites. She decided to have a cup of tea and then go to see Wyn.

A Visitor

Cobridge House was quiet when she arrived. There were no parked cars and everywhere seemed deserted. She went to the back door and knocked. It took some time before Wyn answered, looking a little flustered.

'Oh, Paula. Is everything all right? You look troubled. Come in. I'm afraid I'm rather busy, but you can sit and chat while I'm working.'

Paula shrugged.

'I'm not sure. The hospital didn't say all was as well as can be expected. They told me to go in tomorrow and speak to the doctor again. Oh, Wyn, I'm ever so worried about her.' Paula wiped a tear from her eye with the back of her hand.

Wyn put her hand on her niece's shoulder sympathetically.

'Oh, you poor dear. I'm so sorry. I was hoping to go myself soon, but what with the cook being away on holiday, it's all down to me. Sarah's got her day off today as well. I must get the vegetables prepared. I've made a fruit pie for their pudding and now it's a case of seeing if there's enough of everything else. I never know how many there will be for meals until the last minute,' Wyn said, then shook her head. 'Sorry, I'm blathering on.'

Paula smiled.

'It's all right, Wyn. I'm glad you have plenty to do. Well, I have, too, of course, but it's a bit quiet at home. It's strange coming home to an empty house. I was actually wondering if William might be able to give me a lift to the hospital tomorrow. I daren't ask to leave school early again. I was in real trouble with the headmaster this morning. It makes me so late if I catch the second bus to the hospital. Do you think it's an awful cheek?' she asked her aunt.

'William's been out all day. I think he's at the factory. I heard whispers that he might be joining the firm. His father was looking very pleased this morning any road, when they all went off.'

'I suppose that means he wouldn't be around to take me, anyway. Not to worry,' Paula said, disappointed that she wouldn't see him.

'I'll mention it if I get the chance. You never know what's happening in this place. Now, are you eating properly?'

'Of course. I'm still wading through the remains of the lamb. It is still safe to eat, isn't it?' she asked, concerned.

'I should think so. I would suggest you could stay here, but I'm serving as well as cooking.'

'Perhaps I should stay and help you.' Paula laughed. 'Mind you, I'd probably tip soup all over them and William would die of embarrassment.'

'Soup!' Wyn shrieked. 'I haven't made the soup.'

Paula giggled as Wyn began to dash around the kitchen, grabbing vegetables from here and there.

'You should get William to help,' she

suggested. 'He's a dab hand with a potato peeler.'

'William is? I can't believe that.'

'He knew how to cook the roast.' There was a noise outside the door.

'That sounds like someone coming in. I'd better go and see if I'm expected to make tea as well as everything else,' Wyn said.

'I'd better go and leave you to it.'

'Stay a moment. I might be making a pot of tea and you'd probably like a cup.'

'It's all right. I have a lot to do. I'll give you a call tomorrow after the hospital,' Paula said.

Wyn nodded and went to see about her duties. Paula went home and began to work. At least the fire had lit more easily today, so it was beginning to get warm in the room.

She was in the middle of writing more cards when someone knocked at the door. Mrs Jones, she thought. Oh dear, it was an interruption she could do without, kind though the woman was. Pushing a stray hair out of her eyes, she went to open the door.

'Oh, William,' she said in surprise. 'Sorry, I wasn't expecting to see you. Come in, though the place is a bit of a mess.'

'I came to see you, not how tidy the house is looking. How are you?' he asked.

'All right, I suppose.'

'And your mother?'

'Well, yes, I think she's fine for the moment. I do have a problem at school, though. But forget all that for now. I hear you are thinking of starting work at the factory,' Paula said.

'Looks like it. There seem to be a few projects I can involved in. I'm pretty useless, actually. Everyone seems to have talents for something. All I can do is talk.' William looked sheepish.

'And peel potatoes.' Paula laughed. 'I enjoyed the meal on Sunday. And I shall tonight.'

'You're still eating the cold meat? Oh, dear. Poor you. I should take you out for supper.'

'I have work to do. The cards went down really well. The children all wrote much more neatly than usual, too,' she added.

'So tell me about your problems,' William prompted.

She recounted the headmaster's unpleasant attitude and he was appalled.

'You wouldn't look for another job, would you?' he asked.

'Not likely. I love my work and the children. I owe it to them to make the most of what little education they can get. They'll all have to leave school early to get work and help support their families.'

'So, do you think the head is diverting school funds for something other than the children?'

'He could be.' She told him about the row of new books. 'I don't really know what he does all day. He's never working when I go in there. He pretends to be busy but you can tell he isn't.'

'Perhaps I should pay him a visit one

day and pretend I'm an inspector or something.' William suggested.

Paula giggled.

'It would be a lovely idea, but you're much too young,' she told him.

'How old do you have to be?

'Probably at least ninety.'

'I could wear a false moustache and dust my hair with flour. I shall think of something. Perhaps my father could do it. He's not ninety, though. No, I'll think again. Now, you need to eat. What are you having for supper?'

'Cold meat and bread and butter.'

'That's terrible. How about I fetch some fish and chips for both of us?'

'Fish and chips!' Paula exclaimed. 'But Wyn's been busy cooking all afternoon. She's expecting you for dinner.'

'I said I was coming to see you, so she'll guess I won't be back. Clear your things away and I'll be back soon,' he told her.

'Please don't worry about me. I'll be fine with the meat. I still can't associate you with fish and chips.'

'I love them. A rare treat. Anyway, I want to share supper with you. Is that all right? Now, you have ten minutes to finish what you're doing and clear a space for us to eat.' He kissed the top of her head, making her cheeks turn pink and causing a wide smile to lighten her face. 'That's better. You look lovely when you smile.'

He left and she finished the cards then did as she was told. It was a pleasant, relaxed evening. She talked about her work at school and he spoke of his plans at the factory. She was intrigued by his new ideas of Coronation memorabilia.

'I suppose there's bound to be masses of stuff around. There were quite a few things for the Festival of Britain last year. Mum got me one of the special crowns they produced and I did see other stuff in the shops,' she told him brightly.

'This is going to be massive. I'm taking charge of the marketing and have to visit manufacturers of the lithographs. It makes sense to use the lines they already make and adapt them for the purpose,' William said confidently.

Paula was impressed.

'It sounds really interesting. When do you start?'

'Well, as soon as I like, really. But I haven't told you the most exciting thing. My father is buying me a car. I hope to collect it tomorrow. It's a modest, small thing but it's my own vehicle and means I can drive you around whenever I want. No more cadging Mother's car and getting into trouble for being late back.'

'How wonderful. I was actually going to be cheeky and ask if there was any chance you could give me a lift to the hospital tomorrow after school, but if you're working . . . ' her voice trailed off.

'If I've got my new car in time, there's no problem. I shall probably be visiting other companies and driving around anyway, much of the time. I can easily fit a few little extra trips into my day.'

'I wouldn't ask except I have to see the doctor again. I'm so worried about my mother.' She gave a start. She hadn't even thought about her poor mother for some time with chatting to William so easily. She was immediately contrite. 'I'm sorry. I've been chatting on and forgot where my thoughts should really be.'

'Wyn mentioned how upset you were. I was trying to cheer you up and not let you worry so much. Talk about it if you like.'

She did and managed to voice her greatest fears. He was a wonderful listener and a great comfort.

'I'm sorry to go on so long.'

'You really needed to talk it through. Wyn was really worried about you. That's why I came round. So don't fear, she wasn't expecting me back for dinner.'

'You're a lovely man. Thank you. So thoughtful.'

'Now that's a first for anyone to say about William Cobridge. He's always been considered the world's number one brat and an utter snob.' William laughed loudly.

'I had heard the rumours. So what changed you?'

'Appalachia. Well, some parts of it.'

'I'm not entirely sure where that is. On the eastern side of America?' she asked.

William nodded.

'It was the southern part that was so distressing. Look, I haven't told anyone about it all. I didn't think I could face the memories, but if you can bear to listen, I'd like to tell you. I need to get it out of my system,' he said, and Paula nodded.

'Go ahead. I'm flattered you can talk to me.'

He began by telling her about the rows he'd had with his mother. He'd considered her family some way beneath him and his father. Paula had heard the story of Nellie's rise to fame

189

and how she had overcome so many problems to be where she was today. Anyway, it was fairly common knowledge in the area and something that had never been hidden.

William continued.

'I went off to Cambridge, believing myself to be a cut above the rest. I quickly realised I wasn't any different to the majority of people there. Many of them came from much better backgrounds than I did, though I never admitted it to anyone. I visited the homes of quite a few of the chaps, but didn't invite them back to mine. Besides, my sister was small. I was rather prudish about it. It seemed wrong for someone of my parents' age. So, I didn't think our place was good enough for some of my friends.'

'But your home is wonderful,' Paula said.

'Compared to what? You should see the place my brother-in-law comes from. Dalmere Hall is amazing. Anyway, I didn't think I'd ever soil my superior self by entering the family firm, and my father suggested the trip to America to give me time to decide what I wanted to do,' he said.

'You told me a bit about New York.'

'That was all fine. When I travelled south, I'd assumed everywhere would be the same. But it wasn't. We may think some of our area is deprived, but you realise you've seen nothing like deprivation once you've seen the way they live. Practically cardboard boxes as homes for whole families. Grovelling round scrap heaps for bits of food.' He shuddered and went quiet.

'Why was it so bad there?'

'Collapse of various industries. Mining under terrible conditions. Poor pay. Unemployment.'

'But that happens here, too. There must have been something more?' Paula asked.

'It was the racial segregation. White people could go anywhere, do anything. The black people weren't allowed to ride on the same buses, go to the same schools, eat in the same restaurants. A black women went to buy groceries and was hurled out of the store. Literally hurled out and thrown to the ground. I was appalled.'

Paula gasped.

'I can imagine. What happened?'

'Nothing. She got up and ran away, her head bleeding and nobody even tried to help her. Her blood was red, just the same as all of us. It really made me think. I followed her a little way to make sure she found her way home. I should never have done that. I was cornered.' William paused, remembering the horrors.

'Goodness. It must have been terrifying,' Paula consoled.

'They stripped my clothes off me. Took my wallet and passport. I was carrying all of my money with me. I realise now that I was foolish in carrying it, but I'd thought it might be safer than leaving it somewhere I didn't think was secure. I had no money and they slashed my arm with a knife. I really thought they were going to kill me and I raised my arm to protect my face. I still have the scar. I haven't let anyone see it yet. They went off wearing my jacket and trousers and laughing all the way.'

'Thank heavens they didn't kill you. They could have done.' Paula was finding the story difficult to listen to, but knew she must.

'Easily,' William agreed. 'But I realised that the recriminations for killing a white man could have led to racial riots, and who knows what else. It was a lesson that brought me down to earth. I walked back to where I was staying, barefoot and with blood streaming down my arm. I was near to despair.

'I was staying in a scruffy, cheap hotel having some stupid idea that it might help me see what things were really like. My first mistake. They were less than sympathetic. Because I had no money left, I had to find work in various kitchens to pay my bill. Fortunately, once I'd paid up, I was then able to save just enough to get my rail fare back to New York, where I met up with my father's friends again. They organised a new passport through the Embassy and loaned me some money. I swore them to secrecy about what had happened. I had left my ticket for the return trip with them, fortunately. My father had given me plenty of money to go away with and was pretty shocked when I said it was all gone.'

'Surely they understood when you told them what happened?' Paula asked in disbelief.

'I haven't told them. I could never admit I'd been so utterly foolish and irresponsible.' William looked ashamed.

'But you managed. You found work and got back home.'

'I have never worked so hard in my life. I had hardly any sleep. They paid so little, it took several weeks for me to get enough money to return to New York. I even sold most of my clothes that were left in the hotel. I just kept the minimum I could manage. I had to find somewhere else to stay and I was sleeping in a sort of shed along with several other men.'

'Heavens. What an experience. So now you're not a snob and you can appreciate what you have.'

William nodded.

'Exactly. But, please don't tell anyone. I'm so ashamed of the whole episode,' he confided.

'Will you let me see your scar?' Paula asked.

He rolled up his shirt sleeve and revealed a long red scar which stretched from his elbow almost to his wrist.

'Good heavens. You were lucky it didn't sever an artery!' she exclaimed.

'Like I said, I put my arm up to protect my face and so it caught the outside of it. I think my mother will have a fit when she finally sees it.'

'You should write an account of your adventures. A lesson you should never forget.'

'Forget?' he said sadly. 'As if I could ever forget. It haunts my dreams every night. This is the first time I could bring myself to speak of it to another living soul. Keeping it to myself has been so hard. I've wanted to speak about it but didn't dare, especially not to my parents.'

William looked close to tears.

'My poor love. How terrible. But you came out of it and probably as a much nicer person.' Paula got up and went to put her arms round him. She kissed the top of his head.

They drank tea and gradually William calmed down, collected his thoughts and was returning to normal. Paula felt quite at a loss to know what to say to comfort him.

'I'll do my best to be outside school tomorrow afternoon,' he promised. 'Look out for a small black car with a beige hood. If I can't get there by then, will you be able to catch a bus?'

'I can, of course. It will have to be a later one, as I daren't ask to leave early again. The headmaster certainly wouldn't allow it.'

'I'll do my best. Thank you for listening.'

He took her in his arms and pulled her close. She could feel the tension in his body, but he slowly began to relax.

'You called me your love. Did you mean it?' he asked.

'I think I did.' She smiled at him as he kissed her again.

A Girl In Love

It was a long day at school for Paula. Her mind was drifting in many directions and away from her pupils most of the time. She set them a story to write so she could leave them to get on with it on their own.

She kept thinking of William and the dreadful tale he had told her, and then it was her mother occupying her mind. The coming interview with the doctor scared her, dreading what she might hear.

Automatically, she marked the children's sums from the morning to give her something less to do that evening. At last the school bell rang for the end of lessons and she could help the children into their coats to go home. She kept looking towards the gate, hoping to see a small black car parked, but it was not there.

She felt desperately disappointed, not least because it meant a long wait at the bus stop and a late return home. She would have loved to see William, of course, but it was the hospital journey that was now occupying her mind. She went out to wait for the bus, partly to be out of the way in case the headmaster should seek her out again, and also in case William did arrive late and could see her easily.

* * *

Paula walked into the large hospital building and along the already too-familiar corridors. Dark green and cream. She would never see those colours again without thinking of this place. William had not turned up to give her a lift to the hospital, so she was later to arrive than she had hoped.

She knocked at the sister's office door and waited, but clearly she was not there. She looked into the ward and saw the screens were still around her mother's bed. She hesitated. Should she go and see her mother or would it cause trouble? You just never knew.

'Ah, Miss Frost. Come to the office.' The sister seemed to sail towards her, the starched white hat floating somewhere behind her. 'Your mother is still resting, I'm glad to say.'

'But is she making progress? It surely isn't normal for her to be asleep so much?'

'We're keeping her mildly sedated until she has properly begun the healing process. It's taking time and she is not getting better as quickly as we should like.'

'Will I be able to speak to her doctor?' Paula asked.

'I'm afraid he is busy in theatre but he has authorised me to discuss her treatment plan with you. You need to be prepared. I am sorry to say that some of the tissue that was removed was cancerous.'

Paula blanched and swayed on her

chair. The nurse put out a firm hand to steady her before continuing.

'Now, this doesn't mean it is fatal, so stop thinking that way. We think most of the tissue has been removed and, in any case, there are treatments we shall try and your mother should have a good few years of life ahead. You will need to be strong for her. I don't want you to go to her with gloom and doom on your face. Positive thought. That's what we need.'

Paula's mouth was dry and she couldn't trust herself to speak. She squeaked,

'Can I have some water, please?'

The nurse reached for a jug on her desk and poured a glass of water. After a few sips, Paula felt she could speak again.

'So you're saying she could have treatment?' she asked, struggling to hold back her tears.

The sister nodded.

'We hope so. And you mustn't think of it as a sentence. It should all be cleared if the interventions have been successful. Now, when you have recovered yourself, perhaps you would like to see her for a few minutes? Try not to let her see that you're upset. If you don't think you can manage that, then come again tomorrow.'

'No, of course I want to see her now. But I don't want her to be told about this dreadful disease. Can you keep it from her?'

'I think she already suspects. She is an intelligent woman and must realise that things aren't going so well. But, it's up to you how you manage it. Can you cope?' The nurse looked doubtful.

'I'll be fine. We are very close, you see, there's only the two of us. My father was killed in the war,' Paula confided.

'I'm sorry. It must be difficult for you. You're a teacher, aren't you? You mentioned it before and your mother also told me. She's very proud of you.'

'Thank you.' Paula sipped some more water and put the glass down. 'I'd like to see her now.'

Paula followed the sister to her mother's bedside. She swallowed hard and dug her fingernails into her palms to stop herself from crying. Her mother seemed to have shrunk to nothing and looked so terribly frail.

'Hello, Mum. Sister has let me come to see you, although visitors are not really allowed just now. I told her what a busy life I have.' She smiled and took her mother's limp hand. 'Are you feeling any better?'

'I think so, dear. I'm just so very weak. I feel as if there's an elephant sitting on my chest. I'm a bit sore, but they're wonderful here. They are all looking after me so well. How are you?' her mother asked.

'I'm fine. Looking after myself and even lighting the fire.' Why did I say that, Paula thought? Ridiculous.

'Good. It's not easy that grate.' Olive smiled.

'I'm glad you said that. I did have a fight with it the first day.'

'How are the children at school? I

hope they're being good.'

'Oh, they really are. I have been making work cards for them and they are all so thrilled. It will save me a lot of time in the future, once I've done them all,' Paula told Olive proudly.

'I always said you should. But . . . ' her mother's voice tailed away.

'Don't try to talk. You're getting too tired,' Paula said.

Olive closed her eyes and lay back. Paula talked for a little while longer, recounting silly stories about her pupils, the way she usually did each evening at home. She paused and saw one of the nurses coming to the bedside.

'Your mother should rest now. You can come again tomorrow if you can manage it.'

'Thank you, nurse.' She whispered goodnight, but her mother didn't hear, she was so deeply asleep. Paula crept out of the ward, nodded at the sister and went back along the cream and dark green corridors.

She felt weak, tearful and exhausted.

She looked at her watch. There was half an hour before the next bus. It would be close to seven o'clock before she was home again. She pulled her coat around her and set off to the bus stop.

'Paula? Wait.' Miracles did happen. William was waiting for her, standing by his new car.

'I'm so sorry I wasn't there for you. I couldn't get the car till this afternoon and by the time the paperwork was all completed, I'd missed you. Come on. At least I can drive you back home again.'

'Oh, William. Thank you. Thank you so much.' He helped her into the passenger seat and closed the door. By the time he reached the driving seat, floods of tears were pouring down her cheeks. She sobbed and couldn't stop.

'What is it, darling? Your mother?' William asked softly.

Paula nodded, unable to speak.

'Is she . . . is she . . . ?' He couldn't say the word.

'They say she has cancer. It's not the

worst sort and can be treated, but it's going to be so hard keeping it from her,' she confided.

'Perhaps you won't need to. Perhaps she already knows.' He put a comforting arm around her and held her as close as a small car would allow. 'Let's get you home.'

He started the car and drove carefully, not taking risks with the unfamiliar controls. It took only fifteen minutes to reach her street.

'I was wondering if I should call to tell Auntie Wyn?'

'I can drive you there if you like. Then I'll take you back home again. You're much too exhausted to walk anywhere.'

* * *

Wyn had prepared the family's dinner by the time they arrived at Cobridge House, so she was able to relax. Obviously, she was very concerned on hearing the news, but did her best to cheer up her niece.

'I was wondering if you could give Paula something to eat?' William asked. 'She can have my portion if there isn't enough. It's much too late for her to begin cooking anything when she gets home. I'm worried she may not be eating properly.'

'There's a stew for dinner. I made plenty so I'm sure we can spare her a plate of it.'

'I couldn't,' Paula protested. 'Besides, there's still some cold meat left.'

'We'll both have some here with you, if you don't mind,' William asked Wyn. 'Then I can drive Paula home afterwards. Make sure she gets some rest.'

'Very well, sir, if that's what you'd like.'

'You're both very kind. You mustn't tell Mum when you see her, Wyn. I don't want her to know about the cancer. She'll be very upset.'

'I doubt you'll keep it from her. You know your mother.'

It was warm and cosy in the big

kitchen and gradually Paula began to relax. William seemed perfectly at ease, eating at what had always been the servants' table. Wyn seemed not to mind him being there and even called him William at one point. She apologised but he laughed it off.

'No need for formality here. It's only my father who would be shocked. The way he was brought up, you know. But everything's changing now, isn't it?'

It was only later, when she was falling into an exhausted sleep that Paula remembered something. William had called her darling. It gave her a warm glow.

The next few weeks seemed to fall into a pattern of school, hospital visits, lightened by a few evenings spent with William. They often walked in the local park and he told stories of his family and their associations with the place.

Their friendship was growing and when she had time to pause and think about it, she sensed it was even a growing love between them. His parents had invited her for tea and she had enjoyed meeting them. She got a definite feeling that she had Nellie's approval at least, but it was harder to read James Cobridge. William said that he rarely showed much emotion, but that he could tell that his father had liked her.

Keeping the information about cancer a secret from her mother was difficult. Olive was having treatment that was unpleasant and made her feel sick much of the time. But though she couldn't see it herself, the doctors assured Paula that there were signs of improvement.

She began to make plans for her mother's return home. Unfortunately, the Easter holiday from school had come and gone so her hopes of having time to look after her mother had passed. She had discovered that they could have a district nurse to call a few times during the week, but it still meant long periods when her mother would be left alone.

'Can I come with you to visit your

mother one evening?' William asked, much to Paula's surprise. 'I think it might cheer her up to see someone different.'

'That's kind of you, but I'm not sure how she might feel. She's aware of looking well below her old self.'

'Ask her. I've been so involved all the way through. I'd like to reassure her that I am looking after you just a little. I want her to know that I am serious about you. This isn't some passing thing.'

Paula smiled.

'Oh, William. You are a wonderful man. You've been so kind to me.'

'It's only because I care for you so much. Paula, I want . . . '

'Don't say any more. I can't think past the next few weeks. But thank you.'

'Are you trying to say that you don't care for me? I can't believe that.' William looked hurt.

'Of course I care. Very much. But I have to prioritise my mother's needs before I can think about us and whatever future we may or may not have,' Paula told him.

'I see. Well, please know that I love you and when you feel ready to listen to me, I want to ask you to marry me.'

'Marry you? Oh, William.' Paula felt tears brimming on hearing the words she had longed to hear. 'How wonderful! But you do know I have to put my mother first. I owe it to her after all she has done for me. I can't be selfish and be excited about being married and moving away from her.'

'But you would say yes, if things were different?' he asked.

'I'm sure I would. But it isn't fair to keep you waiting for as long as it might take. You could be having a busy social life instead of spending hours waiting outside the hospital for me.'

'Precisely why I am asking to come with you to visit your mother. You sound as if you're ashamed of me.'

'Now you're being ridiculous. It's surely you who might be ashamed of me.'

It was a conversation going nowhere and suddenly they both began to laugh. He pulled her close and kissed her.

'I am serious, Paula. I've grown to love you very much, for everything you are. A beautiful, caring woman with so many talents. I am sure your mother must be an equally lovely lady and I want to get to know her. And I suspect there was a yes hidden away there. A 'yes' to 'will you marry me?''

'I suppose so.'

'You don't sound very enthusiastic.'

'Don't go round that circle again.' She laughed. 'Are you really sure? I mean, we've only really been seeing each other for a few months.'

'Apart from knowing you most of my life, you mean? I think I knew from that first night we went out for dinner. Not exactly love at first sight, as we'd known each other as children. I just didn't want to rush you into anything. There's nobody else for me, now or ever. So, what do you say? Can you possibly love me as much as I love you?' William looked at her, searching her eyes for her answer.

'Yes,' she called loudly. 'Yes, yes, yes. I'd be honoured to marry you. But — '

He prevented her from saying anything more by covering her lovely mouth with his kisses.

'Can I tell my parents? Please say I can. And your aunt, of course. And if I come to see your mother, I can even ask formally for your hand. You never know, preparing for a wedding might help her get better even more quickly. Motivation. That could be the key to it all.'

'It could be much too soon. And it might have the opposite effect. She could be frightened that she will be left alone,' Paula pointed out sensibly.

'I'll think of some sort of a plan. Don't worry. Leave it with me. Now, home for you, my girl. You need to get some rest before tomorrow. It could be a big day for us.'

'Why? It's a Saturday so I don't have to go to school.'

'I shall be collecting you after

breakfast. We have some shopping to do.'

'But I have to do the washing and clean the house. It's my only chance.'

'More important than buying an engagement ring?'

'If I don't have any clean clothes to wear next week, it might well be,' Paula pointed out.

'We'll buy you some new clothes.'

'William, be sensible. I can't just go buying new things like that. There are still bills to pay and I do have to wash everything anyway. What sort of wife will I ever be if I buy new things all the time, rather than ever doing any washing?' She laughed.

'My wife will never have to do any of that. We shall employ servants to do it,' he told her proudly.

'And where does the money come from to do all that?'

'I shall be earning it. Lots of it. My plans for the company are going really well. I'll tell you all about it another time. I'll leave you here in the morning to do everything and collect you after an early lunch. Then we shall visit your mother and after that, shopping. I shall take you out for a celebratory dinner in the evening.'

Paula laughed with pleasure. Despite the troubles hanging over her, for just a few minutes she was a girl in love with her handsome fiancé.

'It sounds like quite a day. But are you certain you're not rushing into this? Oh, I do love you, William.'

'Thank goodness for that. I love and adore you. Rushing into it? Of course not. Good night, my darling Paula.'

'Goodnight, my darling William.'

Floating somewhere quite new to her, she went inside the house. Strangely, it no longer felt empty.

A Problem Shared

William drove back to Cobridge House. He had a plan. He went straight to the kitchen to see Wyn. Fortunately, she was in her housekeeper's sitting room, having finished work for the day. He knocked at her door and went into the cosy room.

'Oh, Mr William. Sorry,' she said, pulling her feet down from the stool where she'd been resting them.

'No, please don't move. I wondered if I might have a talk to you?'

'Of course. It isn't my sister, is it?'

'Not really. This is confidential and I would appreciate it if you don't speak of it to anyone just yet.' Wyn nodded, looking intrigued. 'I've asked Paula to marry me and she has said yes.'

'Oh, William, that's wonderful. That's lovely. But I suppose you haven't spoken to your parents yet, and nor has anything been said to my sister?'

'That's right. I was wondering if you would visit Mrs Frost tomorrow? I want to buy a ring for Paula and take her out to dinner. Of course, her priority as always is to visit her mother, but I thought if you could visit, that would release Paula for once. I can ask Mother to get someone in to help here, if it's difficult.'

'No, it's fine. There's no event planned tomorrow evening and everyone else is here on duty. I'm due several days off. Can I ask when you would plan to marry?'

'Not too soon. Paula is worried about leaving her mother, of course, so I'm not pressing her to do anything she is less than comfortable with.'

'Very wise. My niece knows her own mind and would resist being forced into anything she didn't like. Well, I can only say congratulations and I hope you will be very happy. I am delighted.' Wyn beamed.

'Thank you, Wyn. I'll leave you in

peace, now. And remember not to say a word to anyone just yet,' he reminded her.

'Of course not.'

After he had left, she sat smiling. It was lovely to think Paula would be happy and her future settled. All the same, the problem of Olive being left alone was a big one. Perhaps she might give up her job and go to look after her. It was her sister's own house so it might provide a solution.

Once Olive was on her feet again, she might be able to find another job of some sort to provide an income for the pair of them. There was such a lot to think about, but the idea had been simmering in her mind for many years.

Wyn arrived at the hospital the following day. It had been a while since she had seen her sister and she was pleased to see some signs of improvement.

'Wyn, how lovely to see you. Does Paula know you are here? I'd like her to have a day off, but she's so very loyal in visiting me every day she possibly can,' Olive said.

'Yes. Paula has gone out with William. I said I'd like to see you and I had some time off, so it's all worked out well,' her sister replied.

'Thank you. It's good to see you. I am so worried about Paula. She's looking quite exhausted.' Olive paused as if wondering what to say. Wyn sat quietly, thinking her sister was weary. 'Can I speak in confidence, Wyn?'

'Course you can, love. What is it?'

'Well, I don't want Paula to know, but I think it's cancer that's been keeping me here for so long. The treatment I've been having, well, it isn't normal for what I've had done. They haven't told me anything, but I'm sure I'm right. I really don't want Paula even more worried than she is at present. Promise you won't say anything?'

Wyn stared at her sister and took her hand. What should she say? That Paula had known all along? Perhaps the hospital hadn't said anything to Olive in case they scared her too much and she gave up trying. It had happened before, she knew very well. But now, she needed to reassure her sister and then perhaps tell Paula that her mother knew what was wrong with her.

'You mustn't worry about Paula. She's a strong woman. I think you might be getting a visit from William tomorrow. He's been bringing Paula to the hospital most evenings and waiting outside. I think it will be nice for both of you to get to know each other.'

'I look such a fright, though. I might scare him off.' Olive said with a laugh.

'Nonsense. You'll be fine.'

'I was wondering how they are getting on. What do you think? Paula won't say too much, but she might not want to worry me. They seem to see quite a lot of each other.'

'Oh, they get on very well. Very well indeed.' Wyn had to bite her tongue or she might let slip the news William had given her the previous evening.

'I just hope she isn't getting out of

her depth with him. That family live on a different scale to us. Well, you know better than anyone. We've had such a quiet life and Paula's got very little experience. I don't want to set too much store by this relationship.'

Wyn smiled and desperately wanted to change the subject before she let something slip.

'Oh, I almost forgot. I made you a little salmon sandwich. I know how much you used to like salmon and we had some for dinner last evening. Here you are. Will you have it now?' Wyn handed her the sandwich.

'How delicious. Thank you. I think I will. They'll be bringing cups of tea round soon.' Olive sat up a little and opened the packet. She ate the sandwich eagerly. 'That was the nicest thing I've eaten in weeks.'

'Good. I can send something else in with William tomorrow. A bit of decent food will help make you better.'

'Thanks for coming, Wyn. I'm glad Paula is getting a bit of a break. I hope she's enjoying herself.'

'Oh, I'm certain she will be,' Wyn replied, barely concealing her smile of pleasure at the thought of the news her sister might be getting the next day.

A Shopping Spree

Paula's morning was frantic. She was getting used to doing the housework and washing but she always had so much to fit in. William was arriving at two o'clock and she wanted to be bathed, dressed and ready for the outing. She had forced herself to concentrate on what needed doing rather than dreaming about rings, being engaged to be married and dinners out. As for the future, she could give no heed to that at all.

She just made it as William knocked at the door. He stood there, looking so very handsome and dressed in a smart suit, holding a bunch of flowers. Her heart leapt. Was he really going to marry her? She could hardly believe her luck.

'How lovely. How traditional,' she said, taking the roses. 'Actually, would you think me terribly ungrateful if I asked if we could take them for Mum? She'd love them, I'm sure.'

'No. You're not visiting today.'

'Oh, but . . . ' she began.

'But nothing. Your aunt has gone instead. We are going shopping. And I have more flowers at home to take for your mother tomorrow. Wyn's telling her that we are both going to see her tomorrow. So, our time is our own for the rest of the day.'

It was a day she would always remember. They went to one of the best jeweller's in Hanley and looked at trays of rings that William had already picked out. In the best traditional style, there were no prices to be seen anywhere and so Paula had no idea what she was looking at. If she had, she would certainly have felt inhibited about anyone spending so much money on her.

'Can I really choose any of these?' she whispered.

'Of course. I did think I'd choose one

for you, but then I thought it might be fun for you to choose yourself. You'll be wearing it, after all.'

'I wonder which you would have chosen?' she mused.

'I'll tell you when you've made your choice,' he told her.

'I'm spoiled for choice. They are all so lovely. I quite like this one,' she said, picking out a group of three diamonds in a row. 'But then, this one might suit my finger better. I have quite small hands, don't I?' She put a solitaire on her ring finger and spread out her hand to look. 'This is the one, isn't it?'

'If that's the one you like.'

'Yes. This one.'

William smiled.

'Then I would have made the right choice,' he said, smiling.

The jeweller smiled at the pair and congratulated them. He put the tray back inside the glass case and took the chosen ring and polished it with a soft cloth.

'May I check the size, madam?' he

225

asked. Paula put out her hand and he slid it onto her finger. 'Thank you. That seems a perfect fit. Your fiancé has a good eye.'

'My fiancé. I like the sound of that.' William kissed her as the jeweller took the ring and put it into a box and a pretty bag. He handed it to William and almost gave a bow. William thanked him as they left the shop. Paula hesitated.

'Don't you have to . . . well, pay?'

'My father has an account there.'

'Oh, I see.' She couldn't imagine someone having an account with a jeweller. The grocer or the butcher maybe, but this was a whole new experience. What was she doing marrying into this family? 'I presume your father has given his approval for you to buy this?'

'Of course. I went to the shop this morning to arrange it all.'

'Well, I hope it wasn't too expensive.'

'It doesn't matter. That's why there were no prices showing. I didn't want you to be influenced by thinking they cost too much.'

'Now I feel guilty. Have I chosen something very expensive?' she asked hesitantly.

'Paula, forget it, darling. Forget about having to count every penny. You're with me now.'

He took hold of her hand and led her into one of the larger stores in the town, one she had always thought much too expensive for her. Whatever she said in protest, William interrupted her until she had given in and accepted that he was quite determined to win.

With a surprisingly expert eye, he riffled along the racks of dresses and picked out two that he liked. She was sent to try them on and told to come out of the changing-room to show him. She was trembling inside. How could she accept such extravagance? She had been wearing her newest dress, the one she had bought from a market stall and, as she changed into one of the new dresses William had selected, she could see the huge difference in quality. A gorgeous kingfisher blue dress settled against her body, a perfect fit.

She absolutely loved it. She paraded it before her fiancé, giggling slightly at the new name she had for him.

'Gorgeous,' he said. 'Now the other one.'

Paula tried on the soft peach coloured creation, a colour she had never worn for reasons of impracticality. Again, William's comment was very positive.

'We'll take both of them,' he told the delighted assistant, when Paula had gone back to the changing-room. 'Have them packed, please, and charged to the Cobridge account. We're going to have tea in the restaurant.'

When Paula returned to him, he took her arm and led her to the restaurant and ordered tea.

'You've become very bossy,' she protested.

'Not really. I just didn't want any arguments from you about expense.

Please, just accept that I love you and I want to please you. There's no use having money if you can't enjoy it. Now, would you like a cream horn or a chocolate eclair?'

An Independent Girl

Dinner that evening was at the same restaurant where their first meal together had been. She had changed into the peacock blue dress and felt wonderful. The waiter arrived with champagne and as he opened it, William slipped the diamond ring on to her finger. The other diners applauded as the waiter poured the wine.

'With our compliments, sir, and our congratulations.'

She blushed, more than she had ever blushed before, but her delighted smile proved her happiness. She laughed as the bubbles hit her nose.

'I could get used to this,' she whispered.

'Good. You will need to. We're going to have the happiest of lives. Thank you for agreeing to be my wife. Now, about tomorrow. You're invited to Sunday lunch with my parents and then we shall go to visit your mother in hospital. I hope this all meets with your approval?'

'Do I have any say in the matter?'

'Sorry. Not really. But you are pleased, aren't you?'

'Of course I am. Nothing can spoil this day. You mustn't think you can always organise my life, though. I'm too used to being independent.' She saw his face fall and he looked distressed. 'Sorry, of course I'm thrilled with everything. Tomorrow will be great but it can never quite match up to today. This has been the best day ever.'

She felt extremely nervous about going to the rather formal Sunday lunch at Cobridge House, but both Nellie and James were quite charming and offered their congratulations, welcoming her to the family.

'I'm delighted to see my son settling down at long last. A new job and a fiancée in so short a time. Excellent.' Paula took this as approval and felt

231

more comfortable. She smiled shyly at William and said she felt very lucky. As she was clearing the table, Wyn asked if she might have a word with her niece. The two of them went out to the corridor.

'What is it, Wyn? Was Mum all right yesterday? She didn't mind me not being there, did she?'

'No, love. But I think you should know, she does know what is wrong with her and asked me not to tell you. In my opinion, you'd do better to speak of it. Perhaps not today, with your other news, but bear it in mind for another time.'

'I see. Thank you for telling me, but it's going to be a very difficult discussion,' Paula said thoughtfully.

'I just wanted you to know. Now, go and enjoy the rest of the meal. Cook's made a wonderful dessert today. And I hope your mother is as pleased by the news as the rest of us are. I didn't mention a thing yesterday.'

'Dear Wyn. You're such a good

friend.' She gave her aunt a hug and went back to the table.

At the hospital later, her mother was equally delighted. There was a light in her eyes that had been missing for too long. She loved the ring and Paula's dress and promised she was going to be up and about in time to help organise the wedding. Her daughter held her hand tightly, offering up a small prayer of hope that her words would come true.

'Why the tears?' Olive asked.

'I seem to have been crying every few minutes since Friday night. Tears of joy, of course. I'm a lucky lady.'

'And I'm a lucky man,' William told them both.

'I'm sure you'll be very happy. And thank you for the lovely roses. My favourites. Now, just you make sure you're careful with that ring, Paula. You mustn't leave it lying around at school.'

'Oh, I won't wear it at school. I wouldn't dare.'

'I don't see why not,' William said in

surprise. 'You should let everyone see that you are engaged to me.'

'I might wear it on a chain round my neck, but it might get damaged when I'm working. I couldn't bear that.'

All too soon it was time to return home again. Floating on her cloud of happiness, Paula could scarcely believe that tomorrow she would be back in front of her class at school. It was very hard to concentrate on writing out her cards and planning her lessons. Tomorrow evening, she needed to have a quiet one, not visiting her mother and staying at home on her own.

When she arrived at school the next morning, it was to something of a storm. Two of the teachers greeted her with the news that the headmaster had been taken ill. He had collapsed over the weekend and been rushed to hospital.

Her class came in with lots of tales of their weekend activities. To give herself time to think, she suggested they should all write about what had happened since Friday.

'Then later on, you can each read out your work to the rest of the class.' Most of them settled to work with a will, but one or two sat staring into space. She went to them to ask if they had something to write.

'No, miss. Didn't do nuffin,' was the reply.

'Write down what you had to eat then. You must have eaten something,' she encouraged.

When the results were read out, there was the usual collection of things like shopping, playing in the park and one had a cat that had produced kittens. She felt sad at their sparse lives. There was little or no stimulation at home and, all too often, parents who spared little time for their children. At lunchtime, one of the other teachers had news.

'I just heard. The headmaster's had a heart attack and won't be returning to school. They'll make a new appointment, but not until September. In the meantime, they will be appointing a temporary acting head.'

Paula smiled to herself. Having a new headteacher was something to look forward to, she thought. Maybe now there would be some changes.

The evening felt very flat. After all the excitement of the weekend, it seemed very dull indeed. The only exciting thing was a letter from the telephone company to say that, at long last, the new telephone would be installed in two days. She went to ask Mrs Jones if she would be willing to let the engineers in when Paula was at school. She gave her a progress report on her mother's health and told her of her recent engagement.

'Oh, Paula, how lovely for you. But how will your poor mother manage without you?'

'I expect it will be a long time before we are married. Plenty of time to think about that. I'll drop the key round before I go to work that morning, if that's all right?' she asked.

'You're getting a bit posh having your

own telephone, aren't you?' Mrs Jones enquired.

'It's really for when Mum comes home. She can keep in touch and call for help if she needs it.'

'I can see that. It will be nice to have a telephone nearby. In case of emergencies, you understand.'

'Of course. I'm sure we shall be happy to help in an emergency.' After she had left, Paula felt a little anxious. She hoped they wouldn't be pestered too often by people wanting to use the phone. It would be a bit of a novelty for a while, but if too many people had the number, it could become a burden. All the same, she knew the phone would be very convenient for them.

For William, the daily routine of working was proving to be much more exciting than he could have imagined. James had given him a number of responsibilities and he was rising to the challenge with a degree of interest that surprised even him. He had spent time in each of the departments at the

Cobridge factory and for the first time in his life, was beginning to respect the toil and labour that went into the production of the china he had taken for granted all of his life. He regretted the fact that he had been unable to collect Paula from school and accompany her to the hospital, but his interest in what he needed to do was growing each day.

'I've picked out several items that I think could be the basis for our Coronation memorabilia range,' he told his mother.

Nellie was in charge of all the decorating departments.

'I was wondering if we could produce a smaller item. A small mug of some sort. I read somewhere the councils are all thinking of giving each child in the country a memento of the occasion. It would be very good if it was our china that was selected for some of the places, at least.'

'I doubt they'd want to pay the sort of prices we charge,' Nellie told him.

'I was thinking of something quite small. If we made enough of them, perhaps it could still be profitable. And it would certainly spread our name even further around the world. Just think, in fifty or even sixty years from now, people would be looking for them as souvenirs of the Queen's Jubilee,' William said excitedly.

'If they lasted that long. I can just imagine some of the kids we see running around dropping them before they were ever taken home. I'm really not sure.'

'Please think about it. I'd really like to follow this through. Oh, and there's going to be a big exhibition in the Victoria Hall later in the year. Everyone who is anyone will be exhibiting there,' he went on. 'We need to get a whole range of things ready for it and the wholesalers will all be there, looking for the best range of stuff to buy for the shops. Shall I book us a stand? We could make a few plates called Coronation ware. Whole dinner services for the export market, perhaps. Exclusive designs from Cobridge Fine Bone China.'

Nellie smiled at her son, unable to believe he was the same man who had left them for university four years ago.

'I'm proud of you, William. You've really settled here. I promise, I will certainly give some thought to your ideas,' she told him.

William beamed.

'Thank you, Mother. I feel I am at last beginning to make a contribution. Do you think Father will agree to put on a show at the exhibition?'

'I should think so. Especially if you take over the organisation of it all.'

'Oh, I will. I have lots of ideas. A big stand, covered in dark blue velvet and swags to cover a raised area. Or do you think red velvet might look better, perhaps? Then there will be large photographs of people working and pictures of all our china — '

'Slow down. It's months away yet and we haven't even got a range of china sorted out. But it's wonderful to see you so keen,' Nellie said, laughing at his enthusiasm.

'I can't wait to tell Paula about it,' he said.

'We'll have to decide about the wedding soon, too. I don't want to find I'm involved in so many other things and then you suddenly spring it on me. And have you thought where you will live?'

'Not really. In fact we haven't talked much about the future at all. I know she still has concerns about her mother being left alone, if she ever comes out of hospital.'

'I expect there will be plenty of time. You should enjoy the coming weeks and just being together. She's a lovely girl. We've both come to like her very much.'

'I'm glad you approve. Not that it would make any difference if you didn't.'

A Vocation

Over the weeks, as the summer gradually crept in, Paula's mother was beginning to improve daily and was becoming restless about the time she had been away from home. At last, the powers that be decided she was well enough to be moved to a convalescent home. It would be an impossible journey for Paula to manage and they had to agree that she would visit only once at the weekend. Neither of them had spoken about the cancer that was threatened, but the hospital staff were optimistic it had been contained.

'We hope it's permanent,' the doctor had told Paula, 'and we are hopeful that she will soon improve. We shall need to check her every few months, but I hope you will enjoy a good long time together.'

'Thank you, Doctor.'

That had been a couple of weeks ago and now Olive was looking forward to some changes in her life. Because she was so much better, Paula could only visit during the official hours. It also meant she had very little time to herself and even less time to see William during the week. Feeling exhausted after a long week at school, she arrived at the hospital to see her mother looking troubled.

'What's wrong, Mum? Are you feeling worse?' she asked.

'No, not at all. But there's something I need to tell you. Paula, I wasn't able to speak of it before, but now that things are looking better, I have had cancer.'

'I know, Mum. I've known all along.' She felt her eyes filling with tears. 'But the doctor is optimistic. He feels the treatment has worked and you will enjoy many more years.'

'You naughty girl. Here I have been trying to keep it from you. I asked Wyn not to say anything.'

'So did I. I had to tell someone when I first knew.'

'She's as bad as you are.' Suddenly she laughed and the two of them clung together, their lovely relationship closer than ever. 'There's one thing I wanted to say. I hope you are planning to get married fairly soon. I want to be a part of this event and the sooner the better, I say.'

'We haven't talked about it much. We're both busy and, well, we were not sure how you were going to be and besides that, we don't know where we shall live,' Paula said.

'You can live at home with me. There's plenty of room.'

Paula looked troubled. She could never see William living in their little house. Especially not with her mother. It would never work.

'That's kind of you, Mum,' she said hesitantly.

'But it wouldn't work, would it?'

'I'm afraid not. But don't think about it yet. We haven't made any plans. Now, what will you need me to bring for your holiday?'

'Holiday? Hardly a holiday. But, I know what you're saying.' She proceeded to give her a long list of clothes, shoes and other things she would need for the convalescent home.

'Well, I just hope William will be around to drive me in, with that lot,' she teased. It was so good to see her mother smiling again.

'How's school going?' Olive asked.

'Big changes. We have a lovely new teacher on the staff who is acting headmaster. He's making lots of changes. Even teaching some of our lessons for us so we can have time to do preparations or marking. And he's ordered lots of new things to help us. Evidently the old head had been keeping back the budget for some reason and then spending it on things for his own use.

'We're now getting plenty of supplies like we never had before. Paper, card, paints, you name it. It's all made such a difference. Best of all, we've now got proper workbooks and work cards, so I don't have to spend hours each day writing out my own. He saw the ones I'd done before and found somewhere that supplied them ready made.'

'Thank goodness for that. It must mean you have more time to see William?' Olive asked.

'Not really. He's also busy. He's doing well at the factory. Making plans and organising all sorts of things. But we see each other at the weekends. I'm hoping he'll be able to drive me over to see you.'

The bell rang for the end of visiting. Wearily, Paula got up from the chair and said goodnight.

'You look worn out, love. Why not ask Wyn to come tomorrow and you have a rest?'

'I'll see. Better go or I'll miss the bus. I'll bring your clothes in on Sunday if William can bring me.'

Paula walked down the corridor and straight into William's arms.

'I meant to be here earlier to see your

mother, but I was held up. Anyway, I'm here now to take you home. Or perhaps you'd like some supper first? I bet you haven't eaten properly.'

Over supper in a small restaurant near the hospital, William took her hand.

'You always work much too hard, Paula. Once we're married, you can give up your teaching and be a lady of leisure. Visit your mother, have lunches with friends and after a little while, I hope we shall be able to start a family.'

She stared at him in horror.

'Give up teaching? I'll never do that. I've always wanted to be a teacher and I worked very hard to achieve it. It was even suggested I applied for the temporary headship at school, but I refused it because of Mum. No, William, I still have a good career to look forward to.'

It was as if a bomb had dropped. He stared at her in total disbelief.

'I couldn't allow my wife to go out to work. Not as a teacher. I want a wife who is going to be a wife and not an exhausted wreck when I come home each evening. I don't want you spending every evening marking children's scruffy books.'

Paula glared.

'Then, clearly, I'm not the right wife for you. I love my work and get so much out of every little achievement my children make.'

'What are you saying, Paula? Don't you want to marry me?' he asked outright.

'Not if it means giving up everything I've ever worked for. Teaching is such a huge part of my life. Surely, nobody in their right mind believes a woman should be forced to stay at home and cook and clean, not these days. And teaching isn't just work. It's a vocation. Almost a mission,' she told him firmly.

'But you can't leave it like this. You can't mean it,' William said.

'I love you, William, and of course I do want to marry you. But I certainly don't intend to give up my career.'

They drove back in silence. He came to the door with her and moved as if he was going to follow her inside.

'No, William. We have nothing more to say to each other,' Paula said sadly.

'But this can't be the end. I won't accept it. Here, take your ring back. Please, Paula. I'll see you tomorrow when you've had a good night's sleep.' He put the ring into her hand and turned away.

She quickly shut the door, leaned against it as if she was trying to make sure she kept him outside and almost slumped to the ground. She made some cocoa and took it upstairs to drink in bed.

Was she really willing to risk everything just to keep her job? Did it truly mean so much to her that she could risk losing William, a happy life together and possibly even a family?

She wished her mother was here, in good health and ready to listen. There was nobody else she could speak to. Wyn? Possibly. But Wyn was too involved with the Cobridge family. She probably wouldn't understand.

She fell into an exhausted sleep and woke in the early hours feeling distinctly unwell. She felt sick and went along to the bathroom, sweating but feeling cold at the same time.

She went back to bed and lay there, shivering despite the warm night. Clearly, she had contracted some sort of infection. Come to think of it, several of her pupils had been off school with some sort of stomach upset recently. She hoped she hadn't passed on anything nasty to her mother. An infection on top of everything else would be a disaster.

She was so glad that it was the weekend, and if she could manage to telephone Wyn to arrange for her to visit her mother, that meant she could stay in bed. Her own chores would have to wait. She fell into a deep sleep and awoke to hear the telephone ringing. For a while, she couldn't think what the noise was. She hauled herself out of bed and went down to the hall.

'Paula. Please may I come round to see you?' William asked. 'We really need to talk.'

'I'm afraid I'm not well. Just leave me alone for now. Can you ask Wyn if she will visit Mum? I need to stay in bed today,' she told him.

'I'm coming round. What's wrong with you? You sound terrible.'

'Please don't come. I'm not up to talking.' Before he could say more, Paula put the phone down and crept back to her bed.

Ten minutes later, she heard someone banging on the door. She knew it had to be William, but she couldn't face him. Not only did she feel ill, she certainly did not want any further arguments, not today. She turned over and pulled the pillow over her ears.

She waited for a while and then listened again. He was still there. He was calling through the letter-box.

'I won't go away, Paula. You need help. Please let me in.' She gave a sigh and pulled on her dressing-gown and went downstairs. She was afraid he might try to break in if she left him outside.

'Oh, my poor love. You look awful. Go and sit down. I'll make a drink for you.'

Paula shook her head.

'I don't want anything. I feel sick.'

'Then you must drink some water. Come on. Is there a blanket or a rug somewhere? You're shivering,' William said.

'I'm really quite warm, thank you.'

'You have a temperature. Do you have a thermometer?'

'I don't think so. It makes no difference, though, does it? I've probably got some sort of bug. Some of the children had one last week.'

He fussed around her for a while and could see that she was ready to fall asleep again.

'Do you want to go back to bed?' he asked.

'I think I should. I feel sleepy again.'

252

'Very well. I'll help you upstairs. If you let me take a key home with me, I'll come back later, when you've had a rest.'

'I'll be all right,' she promised.

'I insist. You can't be left all weekend. I'll come back and bring some food with me. I don't suppose you've done any shopping or anything,' he said.

'Please stop being so nice to me. So practical. I told you, it's over. I've given you my reasons. The engagement is over.'

'I won't accept it, Paula. I love you and you love me. There has to be a way around this. We'll talk about it when you're better. And just hold on to the thought. I love you, Paula. I want to marry you more than anything. We'll talk again when you feel better.'

He helped her upstairs, the first time he had seen that part of the house. Her room was pretty but practical. Exactly what he would have expected. He helped her into bed and straightened her blankets.

'I'll put some water beside you. Try to drink it in small sips.'

'Yes, nurse,' she whispered, smiling at the man she knew she loved, the man whom it was going to be impossible to marry if she wanted to keep her job.

'I'll see you later. Is that the key on the hall table?'

'Yes,' she replied, feeling too weak to protest any more.

Too Late?

When William returned home, his first
call was to the kitchen, where Wyn was
doing her housekeeper tasks and
mending.

'Excuse me intruding on you, but I
have just been to see Paula. She's got a
bug of some sort and seems very
unwell. She asked if there was any
chance that you could visit Mrs Frost
this afternoon?'

'Of course, but what's wrong with
her?' Her aunt was worried.

William shrugged.

'I'm not sure. She looks unwell and is
running a temperature. I confess I am
rather worried about her. I have her house
key and I'm going to go round again
later. She's in bed for now. I wondered if
there's anything I can take her to eat?'

'I'll get the cook to put something
together.'

'Thank you. I will come back for it shortly.'

He left the kitchen and went in search of his mother. She was sitting in the drawing room, writing letters.

'Hello, dear. I thought you were seeing Paula today,' Nellie said, resting her pen down.

'I was planning to but she's ill. Mother, can I talk to you?'

'Of course you can. Is there something wrong?'

'I'm afraid so.' He told her about Paula's behaviour the previous evening. Nellie listened to him intently.

'So the final word is that she says she won't marry me if it means she has to give up her teaching. And her school is in such a terrible area. The children are little more than urchins.'

Nellie tutted.

'Oh, William. You never learn, do you? You have to accept that Paula is a woman of high principles. She loves her work, however difficult the circumstances. She is a dedicated teacher with a true calling. I can quite see why she doesn't want to give up her work.'

'But I can't have a wife of mine working so hard and going out of the house every day. She will have a position to uphold,' he said firmly.

'William, stop and think. What am I doing every day? What have I always done all my life? I go out to work,' she reminded her son.

'That's different. You have a respectable job in your husband's own factory. And we have staff here to organise the household,' was his reply.

'And so you consider Paula's job is less respectable?' Nellie looked seriously at her son. 'You need to think carefully about what you are asking. Remember, women no longer want or expect to be totally dependent on their husbands.'

William stared at Nellie in disbelief. He had felt certain she would understand his point of view.

'But you depend on Father, surely?' Nellie shook her head.

'Not financially. I have earned my own wages all through my life. How else was I able to help Lizzie get her decent education? I was never going to ask your father for money for something like that. And I was able to bring your grandmother to live here without feeling I was imposing on your father. I was able to help Ben and Joe, as well, at different times.

'Maybe you should go and talk to your aunt Lizzie. She might help put you straight about how women feel about independence.'

William shook his head, bemused.

'I shall never understand you. Any of you. I thought you would enjoy being looked after. Not to have to work.'

'What, sit around every day and make polite conversation with people you don't particularly like? No, thank you. Those days are long gone, thank goodness. Your father's mother may have enjoyed living like that, but not our generation.

'Perhaps it was the war that finally

258

changed everything. Women often had to do men's work when there was no-one else to do it. They could never go back to being merely ornaments.'

William left her and went to his room. He sat gazing through the window for a long time. The lunch bell rang and he went down to the dining room. Sarah brought in the meal and disappeared again once they were all served.

'You're very quiet, my boy,' James remarked.

'Things on my mind,' William answered. 'Can I ask you something? Did you mind that Mother always worked?'

'Of course not. Where would Cobridge's be now without your mother? We owe much of our success in recent years to her talents.'

'And you didn't want to look after her? Have her at home, always waiting for you at the end of the day?'

James looked startled. He looked at Nellie as if seeking answers.

'No, William. It never occurred to me

259

that your mother would want to stay at home and try to be a lady of leisure. Not in her nature. She even went into work during much of her pregnancy, when she was carrying you. And later with Beth. Now, would you mind telling me why on earth you're asking all these foolish questions?' James said curiously.

William declined to say more, finishing the rest of his meal in near silence. He had much to think about.

★ ★ ★

Before going back to Paula's house, he went for a long walk round the nearby park. The park had associations with many of the family, according to the tales he had heard. Tea taken in the café, boating trips on the lake had all played their part. He and Paula had done few of those things. Most of the time since they had become close, they had been visiting her sick mother. They should have been doing many more things together.

He thought about his aunts and his uncles' wives and what they all did. Daisy worked on the farm that had belonged to her parents; Jenny was still partly a nursemaid, looking after Beth when it was necessary; Lizzie, well, Aunt Lizzie did any number of things, including writing articles, and he had even heard tell that she was writing a book. She had also been a nurse during the war.

So it seemed his ideas of the little wife left at home all day were somewhat out-dated. He wondered why he'd even had those ideas, but they seemed to have always been a part of him.

Perhaps it was the talk of some of his fellow students who had spoken of their mothers having coffee mornings and lunch parties. He assumed that was what went on everywhere.

Clearly he hadn't thought it through. How had he failed to realise that his own mother had always worked? Stupid, prejudiced man, he admonished himself.

He realised he was quite close to his aunt's house and decided to call on the off chance she would be free. He rang the bell and his uncle-in-law, Daniel, opened it.

'Oh, Uncle Daniel, I'm sorry to disturb you,' William said politely.

'It's all right. Come in, we're just having a quiet afternoon. The maid's having time off, hence it was me opening the door.' William followed him to the sitting room, a much smaller, cosier room than the formal drawing-room at Cobridge House. Daniel was scarcely limping these days after his flying accident in the war.

'William. How lovely to see you,' Lizzie said, heaving herself out of her chair. She was expecting their first child in a month or so and claimed she was larger than most whales.

'Please, don't get up,' Williams told her.

They exchanged pleasantries for a while and he politely asked after her health. Finally, he plucked up courage to ask, 'I wondered if I could have a chat with you?'

'Of course. It's been much too long since we saw you. How's Paula?'

'It's partly about Paula. She's not well at the moment, but that's not why I need to talk.'

'Sit down and tell me all about it,' Lizzie coaxed him.

He repeated again the conversation he'd had with Paula about giving up teaching. Before he had said much, Lizzie was scoffing.

'You are joking?' she exploded. 'You mean to say you expected her to give up something she has worked so hard to achieve? What did you expect her to do all day?'

'I'm learning rapidly that I have made a mistake. I just assumed she'd be glad to give up working quite so hard in that awful school. Some of the tales she tells me, well I can't believe such places still exist in 1952.'

'I think you have missed the point. We women certainly like to be loved and cared for, but none of us are dolls these days. The suffragettes didn't fight for the vote so women could sit down all day and be totally passive.'

William nodded.

'So I'm beginning to realise. Mother was saying pretty much the same things. Thank you. I'll have to go to Paula's and see if she'll still speak to me. She called off the engagement last night so I have to build some bridges, I think.'

'I think you certainly do. Good luck.'

They chatted for a while longer. He was fond of his aunt Lizzie and uncle Daniel. He saw them as having a happy marriage and a healthy attitude to life, but again he had missed understanding the female need to work.

'How are you getting on at the factory?' Daniel asked.

'I'm enjoying it, surprisingly. It's good to see you around occasionally.'

'It suits me well enough.' Daniel was in charge of the accounts department at Cobridge's, a position he had taken up soon after he and Lizzie were married.

'I'd better go and see if I can make any progress with Paula. It seems I have a lot of misconceptions and consequently, I've made mistakes.'

'Good luck, William. I hope you're successful. We all like Paula and want you to be happy.'

He walked back to his home, deciding he would then go back to see his Paula and tell her that now he understood.

He just hoped it wasn't too late and that he hadn't truly lost her.

Wyn's Idea

Wyn caught the bus to the hospital and was delighted to see her sister looking much better. They chatted about inconsequential things for a while, until Olive asked her how she thought Paula was looking. Wyn frowned. She didn't want to worry her sister, but she couldn't lie.

'She's got some sort of bug, according to William. I expect it's just something she caught from one of the pupils.'

'I knew there was something wrong last night. She works much too hard and visiting me all the time is taking it out of her. I'm not sure how she'll manage when I get home, if I can't do everything I always have done, and I don't know what will happen when she and William are married. I said they could stay with me but I can see that wouldn't work.'

Wyn spoke up.

'I've had an idea. I am thinking of leaving Cobridge House. They don't really need a full-time housekeeper these days, and besides which, I have had enough of it. Now most of the family have left, I could easily hand in my notice and I'm quite sure they won't miss me.

'This is just an idea, but how would it be if I came to live with you? I could help you when necessary and maybe get a little job somewhere.'

Olive was delighted.

'Oh, Wyn, that sounds wonderful. It really does. Would you really be happy doing that?' she asked.

'I would. We've always got on really well, haven't we? It could be the answer to our worries. I have some money put by which would last me for a while and my pension.'

'I've got my widow's pension. Thank you, Wyn. It's such a relief to me. I never dreamt of anything like this.'

The two sisters sat together for some

time longer, making plans and feeling excited that their futures were getting settled.

'Which of us will tell Paula the news?' Wyn asked.

'You can tell her. You'll see her first,' Olive replied.

'I might phone her to see how she is later on.'

Olive stared at her.

'What do you mean?'

'Oh, didn't you know Paula had a telephone installed?'

'Is there anything else I should know about?' Mrs Frost demanded.

'I don't think so. But you'll love it. It makes life so much easier having it there.'

'A telephone? Me living with a telephone? Infernal machines. I can imagine half the street coming to ask if they can use it,' Olive said.

'You'll soon get used to it. Save you walking into town each week to order meat from the butcher's.'

Olive burst out laughing.

'I won't even have to do that. You'll be doing it for me. You always were a better cook than me, if I'm honest. You've made me very happy, Wyn. Thank you.'

★ ★ ★

William collected a small hamper of food from the cook and put it into his car. He hoped Paula was feeling better, as he felt very inadequate knowing how to cope with illness.

There had always been someone to take charge at home if anyone was unwell. Now, Paula had nobody but him. He let himself into the quiet house and called to Paula.

'Hello? It's me. Are you awake?' he called to her.

'William, I'm in the kitchen. I'm feeling much better. I think I was just exhausted, and then with everything last night, well, I suppose I just collapsed,' she told him.

'Cook's put some things together for

you. I hope you will enjoy them. She's an excellent cook.' He took out several items. Some cooked chicken with a small salad. Fresh rolls and butter. Some slices of smoked salmon. A covered container with some soup.

'What a feast! There's enough to last for days.'

'Not if I help you eat it. I thought it would be nice to share a meal together and talk, if you're up to it, of course.'

'I'm not going to argue any more. I've made my position quite clear,' she said firmly.

'I don't want you to argue. But I would like you to listen to me. I've been thinking a lot and I spoke to my mother and my aunt. They both pointed out a number of things to me. I should have realised that times have changed. Women are individuals not extensions of their husbands. In fact, most of the women I know well all have work to do.

'My mother is probably the main one in all this. She has always worked and my father never questioned it. I've always been rather selfish. It never occurred to me how much work goes on behind the scenes in a home. Meals turn up on time each day, three or four times a day. Laundry is always done and arrives back in my wardrobe. Fires are lit. Somehow, it all just happens.

He went on.

'America did teach me some things, but I think I've let all that slip into the past again. The women who work at the factory are all skilled at what they do but I suppose I thought they work because we need them to perform these complex tasks and they don't always have husbands to look after them.'

'And do you also realise that teaching children is one of these complex tasks? It requires a lot of training and a whole wide range of skills,' Paula asked him.

'I do, Paula. I really do. I am so sorry if you were feeling that I was disparaging about your skills. I never meant it that way at all.

'So, if you will forgive me, please tell

me that we are still engaged and, of course, I realise you must always do as you wish regarding your teaching career.'

Paula beamed.

'After such a speech, how can I say no? I'm pleased you can see my point of view now.'

'Then hold out your hand.' He picked up the engagement ring from the table and slipped it back on her finger. Paula stared at it.

'Thank you, William.'

'And might we talk about the wedding soon? I'd like it to be as soon as we can arrange it,' he told her.

'But there is so much to think about. My mother, for a start. And where would we live?'

'This is just an idea, but would you and your mother both consider living at Cobridge House?'

'Goodness me. It's a generous offer, but I don't think my mother would like to lose her independence. Plus, she'd be uncomfortable if her sister was employed there and she was, well, a sort of guest.'

'Think about it. She would be well looked after while she is convalescing and might decide to move back here when she is fully recovered.'

* * *

They had scarcely begun eating when the phone rang.

'Paula, dear, it's Wyn.'

'Wyn. Is everything all right? Have you seen Mum?'

'She's fine. But we've come up with a suggestion we'd like to put to you. You can say no if you don't like the idea. May I come round and talk to you?'

'Well, of course. William is here. We're having supper.'

'I'll come right away.' She put the phone down, leaving Paula puzzled.

'Wyn's coming round. Some idea they've cooked up between them. My mother and her.'

'Would you like me to leave?'

'No. I'll put the dishes in the sink to soak. Thank your cook for the lovely food. I really enjoyed it and I now feel quite well again. Shall I make some coffee?'

He followed her into the scullery, carrying the dishes.

'I should get used to helping with such chores if we are to be as equals,' he remarked. She laughed as she watched him clumsily stacking the dirty dishes. 'I feel as if you've forgiven me for my thoughtless remarks. I hope I'm right.'

'I suppose so. Why do you think Wyn is coming round at his time of the evening?' There was a knock at the door.

'I hope I'm not intruding. Are you feeling better, dear? Mr William said you were unwell,' her aunt said.

'I think it's about time you dropped the Mister from my name,' William suggested.

'Thank you. If we are to be almost related, I suppose it would be a little

274

odd. Now, your mother and I have been making plans. Subject to your approval, of course, Paula.'

'Go on. I'm intrigued.'

'I have been considering leaving Cobridge House and I have suggested that I move here to live with your mother. It seemed like a good solution. I'll be here to help your mother until she's really got her strength back and then we shall be company for each other. What do you think?'

'That sounds a wonderful idea,' Paula replied. 'I know Mum would love to have you here and I should be happy to know there was someone to be here with her.'

'I must admit, I'm rather pleased with my idea,' Wyn went on. 'It seems a solution to all our problems. And if you don't mind having me here before your wedding, I shall hand in my notice very soon.'

William was listening to the conversation and his face lit up with a broad grin.

'It means we can start planning the wedding properly. And if Paula moves to Cobridge House eventually, it's like swapping one inhabitant for another.'

'I'll have to think about that,' Paula said cautiously. 'I'm still not sure how it would work.'

'It looks as if major changes are on their way all round. We'll discuss it with my parents anyway, as soon as possible.'

'Your first sewing commission could be to make my wedding dress, Wyn. If you're willing, of course.'

'Oh, Paula, it would be my absolute pleasure.'

'This all sounds very promising,' William said. 'Perhaps you would like a lift home, Wyn?'

'We haven't had coffee yet. Shall I make some for all of us? While the kettle's boiling, I can wash out the dishes you brought William, and then you can return them.'

'I'll help you,' Wyn offered. The two women disappeared into the kitchen and William heard them chatting as he sat by himself.

He felt gratified that their problems were gradually being resolved. Now all he had to do was to work out where he and Paula could live when they were married. Perhaps the idea of Cobridge House didn't appeal to her, but he could see no real alternative.

Perhaps his father would agree to buy something for them, like Daniel's father had done for them. But he had the feeling that money was still a little tight at present and this might be asking too much. Odd hints had been made that everything was more restricted than in the past. Hopefully the Coronation, and all it brought to the economy of the area, would be helpful.

The two women returned with the tray of coffee and the hamper containing the clean dishes.

'So, have you got everything organised?' he asked. 'I heard you talking earnestly there.'

'There's such a lot to think about.

I've suggested that Wyn moves here as soon as she has served her notice with your parents. If it's going to happen anyway, we might as well get things moving,' Paula told him.

'My parents will be less enthusiastic than you think about you leaving,' William told them. 'Especially with a wedding happening. They will probably want to offer Cobridge House for the reception, but I suppose it may not be large enough, come to think of it.'

'But I don't want a huge wedding. Please, let's keep this simple and make it our very own special day. Anyway, there are so many more practical things to think about. I'm not sure I want to live at Cobridge House, for a start. I will always think of it as your parents' home, not mine,' Paula pointed out.

'It may be mine one day,' William observed. 'Not for a long time, I hope, but it is something we should think about eventually.'

'Perhaps you could use just a part of it for your home.' Wyn suggested.

'There are plenty of rooms upstairs that are all closed up. I'm sure they could make a nice place for you.'

'But I'd hate to have all my meals in the formal dining room,' Paula objected. 'Changing for dinner every evening and trying to make polite conversation all the time. It's not me at all.'

'Goodness, is that how we seem to you?' William was quiet for a moment. 'Actually, apart from not dressing for dinner any more, I expect you're right. Mother is less formal, but my father is still a bit reserved.'

Wyn was smiling. She still remembered James's shock when the rest of the family decided against dressing for dinner, during and after the war. The tradition had never been resumed, except, of course, when they had formal dinner parties.

William spoke again.

'I suggest you come for lunch tomorrow and we can discuss our plans with my parents. It's coming together nicely, don't you think? Now, if you're ready, Wyn, let's leave Paula to get some rest.'

Wyn collected the hamper and discreetly went to the door, leaving them to say goodnight.

'I'm so pleased we have got things sorted out. I had a terrible night last night. I couldn't bear to think of life without you. Goodnight, my love. I'll come and collect you tomorrow.'

'I need to take Mum's things for the convalescent home, so I'll be grateful for the lift.'

He drew her close and kissed her with a promise of things to come. She felt her heart filling with joy once more. What great excitement the next weeks would bring.

So Much To Do!

It was the middle of August. Wyn had moved to live with her sister and niece. Olive was greatly recovered, though still easily tired and much weaker than she had been. Ever since she had moved in, the house had been a hive of activity with preparations for the wedding. It was now only two days away and Paula was a nervous wreck.

'Calm down, dear. You'll be a bride with bags under your eyes and grey hairs at this rate. Everything's ready. Your dress is lovely. The cake is perfect.'

The cook at Cobridge House had made and decorated it quite superbly. It was a work of art and Wyn had complimented her when she had seen it at her last visit. She was doing her very best to keep the stress away from her sister as well as trying to calm the bride-to-be.

'But the apartment is in a terrible state. It will never be ready for us to move into!' Paula exclaimed.

They had agreed to re-model some of the rooms at Cobridge House to make a self-contained apartment for the newly weds.

'You're going away on honeymoon for two weeks after the wedding so there's plenty of time. I'll go round to make sure everything's in place before you're back.'

'But there's so much to do. Curtains to be hung. Painting to be finished . . . ' Paula began.

'Paula, it will be done. You don't have to concern yourself with these details. Get used to the fact that you're moving into a different world now. A world where things are done for you. All you had to do was approve things that are being purchased for you, and you've done all that.'

'I know you're right. I'm still not used to it. I've always been used to having to save up for things. Buying things from the market because they're cheaper.'

She giggled at the memory of trying on a new dress in the toilets when she first went out with William. She'd never dare to tell him. That particular dress had already begun to look scruffy in comparison to the two dresses he'd bought for her. Quality was quality, it seemed.

'Are you going round to see Daniel and Lizzie again this evening?' her mother asked.

'Yes, just to fix the final details.'

'It's really lovely that he's agreed to give you away. There's rather a shortage of males in our family.'

'I really like them both. And their baby daughter is gorgeous,' Paula said with a smile.

'Perhaps you'll have one of your own before too long,' Wyn suggested.

'I hope not. I'm starting my new job in September. I felt a bit sad saying goodbye to my class, but they would have moved on to another teacher anyway.'

'It's a much nicer school you'll be going to and much nearer home for you. And your little sister-in-law will be there, too.'

'Sister-in-law. Sounds a bit strange to have a six-year-old as a sister-in-law.' Paula giggled.

It had been a bit of a compromise to leave the school she loved, but a job had come up at the school nearest to Cobridge House. She had agreed it was a compromise worth making and she was very happy with it.

Her old school had a good new headmaster who was already putting things right and making sure the budget was spent correctly. She could leave her pupils safe in the knowledge that everything had changed for the better.

Beth was going to start in the junior department in September and everyone had agreed it would be a good move for Paula to teach there.

'I'm not sure how it's going to work having that one in my class. Beth's rather a spoiled child at the moment, but no doubt she'll soon come round.

'Goodness, how my life has changed this year. Those dreadful weeks when I thought I was going to lose you, Mum.'

'One good thing has come out of it, anyway. I got to know my lovely niece so much better,' Wyn said fondly.

* * *

Two days later, wearing a simple white dress and the veil her mother had worn at her own wedding, Paula, with her slightly shaking arm linked with Daniel's, walked up the aisle to meet her groom. He looked handsome in his morning suit and their eyes met, making her nerves disappear completely.

The congregation, much larger than Paula had wanted, were all exquisitely dressed for the occasion. But nothing mattered any more. She was here, making her vows to the man she loved deeply and it might just have been the two of them and the vicar present. She had no more nerves about the day or her future life. The whole family had come together to wish them well.

Nellie held James's hand tightly, her eyes brimming with tears. Their own wedding had been a secret, rather clandestine affair in a registry office, because his parents had disapproved. Now she was the mother of the bridegroom, her own son who was at last showing responsibility for his future.

Lizzie, holding her new baby, waited for Daniel's duties to be finished and for him to sit beside her. Her own wedding had been a grand affair at Dalmere Hall. Daniel's parents had disapproved nearly as much as her sister's in-laws, but had come round to the fact that their son was happy. She couldn't possibly have been happier and knew their lives were the best she could have hoped for.

Daisy and Joe, Nellie's eldest brother, were sitting with their daughter, Sally. His life had turned out to be everything he could have dreamed of. It was a very different life compared to his own childhood and teenage years. He would never have dreamed he could be so happy, all those years ago. He only remembered in his worst nightmares the days when he was working in the dark in that terrible coal mine, trying to help his father cover up the fact he had been injured. He reached for Daisy's hand and smiled at her.

Ben, Nellie's other brother, was sitting with Jenny, the one-time nursemaid at Cobridge House. He was one of the most talented makers of studio pottery in the factory. Their son, Tom, was wriggling beside Beth. Unwillingly, he was acting as page boy and now waited with the little bridesmaid.

Jenny and Ben's lives had been almost finished by the horrors of the war. He had been missing, presumed dead for many months but came back alive. Together, he and his lovely Jenny had worked through it all and they had brought their second child into the world.

Nellie looked round, and thought of her mother. How proud she would have been to see this group of people. They had forgotten the poverty of their past. The constant struggle to put food on the table. Always feeling hungry.

That was all in the past. Now the future awaited for them all and who could tell what lay ahead?

The bride and groom had made their vows. The next generation were beginning their lives.

WHERE THE HEART IS
OUT OF THE BLUE
TOMORROW'S DREAMS
DARE TO LOVE
WHERE LOVE BELONGS
TO LOVE AGAIN